Wild Cat

BL: 3.6 ARpts:5

Tyndale House Publishers, Inc. • Carol Stream, Illinois

STARLIGHT

3

Animal Rescue

Wild Cat

DANDI DALEY MACKALL

Visit Tyndale online at www.tyndale.com.

You can contact Dandi Daley Mackall through her website at www.dandibooks.com.

TYNDALE and Tyndale's quill logo are registered trademarks of Tyndale House Publishers, Inc.

Wild Cat

Designed by Jacqueline L. Nuñez

Edited by Stephanie Rische

Scripture quotations are taken from the *Holy Bible*, New Living Translation, copyright © 1996, 2004, 2007 by Tyndale House Foundation. Used by permission of Tyndale House Publishers, Inc., Carol Stream, Illinois 60188. All rights reserved.

For manufacturing information regarding this product, please call 1-800-323-9400.

ISBN 978-1-4143-1270-5

Printed in the United States of America

16   15
8   7   6   5

ONE

I WISH ANIMALS COULD TALK.

This is what I'm thinking, watching Hank and Dakota unload eight horses they rescued from Happy Horsey Trail Rides.

Happy Horsey? There's nothing happy about these horses. They're skinny, scarred, scraggly, and scared. If they could talk, their stories would probably tear my heart into little pieces.

"Hank! Can I help?" I shout at him. He's trying to get a spotted mare to back down the trailer ramp. She stomps one back leg like she's squishing a snake, then lunges toward the trailer. Her flank is so scabbed over it looks like rough leather.

Hank gets the horse to back halfway down the ramp. I'm about to ask him again if I can help when he yells at me. "Kat! Stay back!"

I don't usually get to help with the horses. I'm in charge of cats. But I've been hoping Hank would make an exception this time. I really want to help these poor horses.

The mare bolts up the ramp again. Hank smooth-talks her. "Come on, gal," he coaxes. My brother—well, he'll officially be my brother as soon as my adoption is final—is 16. If that stubborn horse were a junior high or high school girl instead of a horse, she'd come thundering down the ramp fast as you please to follow Hank. Every girl I know in Nice, Illinois, has a crush on Hank.

Midway on the Pinto's bony rump is a deep brand: HH. Happy Horsey. A jagged scar streaks under the brand like a ghostly underline. I try not to think about how it got there. I wish I could do something to help.

"Quit daydreaming, will you?" Hank shouts. "You're going to get hurt." He and the spotted mare match step for step down the ramp, trotting backward when they touch ground. Then they jog off to the pasture, leaving me in a puff of dust.

I move into the barn. It's a great barn, with stalls in back and a round pen out front that takes up half of the sawdust floor. Everything smells fresh, like the forest. If I were a horse, I'd love it here. In this very barn I touched my first horse, kissed my first cat, and got my first dog bite.

My cat, Kitten, climbs my leg, claws up my back, and settles onto my shoulders, where she curls her scraggly self around my neck. I'm sweaty, so Kitten's shaggy white fur sticks to me. I don't mind. Kitten and I go way back. I found her half-dead in a ditch. She was my first rescue.

Kitten rubs her face against my ear. She purrs, and it sounds like a swarm of locusts. Then, just like that, she digs her claws into my shoulder and springs off.

"Kitten!" I scold. But she's long gone.

Dakota teases me about *Kitten* not being the most creative name in cat history. But since my nickname is Kat, I think "Kitten" is the perfect name for my first rescued cat at Starlight Animal Rescue.

"Look out!" Dakota shouts.

I turn, and I'm nose-to-nose with a scrawny chestnut pony. A wide, raised scar runs the length of his head, splitting it in two. His eyelids sag, and he's bone thin all over.

"Move, Kat! I'm not kidding!" Dakota tugs on the pony's lead rope. But she's leading another horse too, a skinny gray mare who wants to return to the trailer.

I take a couple of steps back from the pony. "Sorry. I just wanted to help."

"Right now you can help by staying out of the way," Dakota says. "You could get hurt." Dakota's 16, like Hank. She could probably pass for Cherokee–she's that exotic looking. I love Dakota like a sister, but she worries about me too much. She freaks out if I break a fingernail. Once people learn I've got cancer, they treat me like I'm made of glass.

I watch Dakota struggle to keep both horses behind her as she leads them through the barn. "The pony's limping," I call to her.

"What?" She starts to turn around. The gray mare tugs sideways, pulling Dakota with her. The poor pony's nearly jerked off his feet.

Hooves. Not feet.

Okay. So I'm not exactly a horsewoman. But neither was Dakota when Ms. Bean, the social worker, dropped her off at Starlight Animal Rescue. That was only a couple of months ago. Now Hank says he couldn't get on without her.

I wonder what that would feel like, to know people couldn't get on without you.

The whole Coolidge family is like one big hall of fame. A doctor, a firefighter, an expert dog trainer, two horse whisperers . . . and me.

"You guys are going to need help with all those horses, you know." I have to shout so Dakota can hear me. She's still making her way to the stalls with both horses.

I tag along. "That pony's favoring his right foreleg, Dakota," I try again.

"I know. We think it's a bowed tendon. The vet examined all the horses before we picked them up. Doc Jim said we'll need to give this one some bute—Butazolodine—until his leg heals." Dakota has control of the horses again. She frowns at me. "Not so close, Kat."

I'm trying to study the pony's forelegs. "His leg doesn't look bowed to me. Are you sure–?"

"Not now. Okay?" Dakota begs.

"You know," I say, hustling to keep up with her, "this is the first time we've taken on so many horses at once."

"You and your first times," Dakota says, shaking her head.

It's true that I love firsts. First snow of the year. First leaf to turn in autumn. (It hasn't happened yet.) First robin in spring. The first time Hank called me "little sis." The first time Kitten purred for me.

Yesterday I heard three cats purr at the same time. I wrote Catman, Hank's cat-loving cousin, about it. Catman knows more about cats than anybody in the whole world. He's even making a movie about cats, a documentary. He and Winnie the Horse Gentler run a pet helpline on the Web. I still haven't met them, even though they're just a couple of states away, in Ohio. But it's hard for people with animals to leave home.

"Kat! Did you hear me?" Dakota yells. She's standing in front of an empty stall, a horse on each side, pulling her in opposite directions. "Will you open the stall door? Please?"

"Oops. Sorry." I slip in front of her and unlatch the door.

"Thanks." Dakota leads the gray mare into the stall. The pony tries to follow. "Stay!" Dakota commands.

"Let me take the pony," I beg.

She hesitates. "I don't know. You could get stepped on."

"By the pony? Poor thing's so skinny, I wouldn't even feel it if he did step on me," I joke. "Besides, I won't get stepped on. Please, Dakota. I really want to help you guys." I reach over to stroke the pony. His neck twitches like a fly's landed on it. He sidesteps.

That's enough for Dakota. "Maybe later. You better ask Popeye and Annie first." Popeye is my dad, Chester Coolidge, and Annie is my mom. Dakota and I are both fosters, but she doesn't call them Mom and Dad like I do.

Dakota unsnaps the lead from the gray horse's halter. The snap startles the pony. He jerks and backs away fast. The rope slips out of Dakota's hand.

Without thinking, I lunge for the pony's lead rope, grabbing it in both fists.

The pony bolts. My hands stay glued to the rope. I jerk forward. My feet fly out from under me. The pony takes off up the stallway.

"Kat!" Dakota screams.

I hit the ground hard. My stomach's a sled as I'm dragged over sawdust.

I hear Dakota's cries behind me. "Kat! Let go of the rope!"

I see my hands on the rope. But they don't belong to me. They won't let go. The pony's tail slaps my arm. I bounce over something. Dirt sprays my face. I barely feel it. I'm numb. I can't see. I close my eyes and wonder if I'll ever see again.

I've heard your whole life flashes before you at a time like this. But my life isn't even a flash. More like a spark. A fizzle. I haven't done anything with my life.

Fear shoots through my bloodstream. I feel it like the cold ink they inject in me before X-rays.

X-rays. IVs. Tests. Cancer. That's how I'm supposed to die.

Not like this.

Two

"WHOA! WHOA, BOY!"

I slide to a stop, inches from the pony's back hooves. My eyes sting when I open them. I shut them fast. The world is spinning as I wait for the pain to catch up with me.

"That's a good boy." It's Hank's voice I hear, coming from miles away. "Kat, are you okay? Let go of the rope."

I uncurl my fingers and roll to my side. Fetal position.

It hurts to breathe. I cough. It hurts even more. Everywhere.

Dakota drops to her knees beside me.

"Kat? Can you hear me? I'm sorry! I didn't . . . Are you . . . ?" She's crying hard.

I want to tell her I'm okay. *Am I?*

"She's bleeding, Hank!" Dakota screams.

"Where's she bleeding?" Hank demands.

That's what *I* want to know. I think of opening my eyes and seeing for myself. But I don't.

"I think it's just her arms," Dakota answers. "Or her hands." She sneezes. *Achoo!*

I smell sawdust. I feel it in my nostrils. *Please don't let me sneeze.* The thought of it makes my sides ache.

Dakota sneezes again.

"Bless you," I whisper. I'm not sure if I've said it out loud or not.

"Kat!" Dakota falls on top of me, hugging me. Then she scoots away, like I'm glass again. "Hank, she blessed my sneeze." Dakota breaks down into sobs.

Is this the first time I've seen her cry?

"Don't move." Hank runs toward the stalls, leading the pony behind him. In seconds he's back. I open my eyes enough to see the tips of his scuffed boots.

"Kat?" Hank says. He squats beside me.

My eyes are watering so much that Hank and Dakota look blurry. "I think I'm okay."

"Don't move till you're sure," Hank warns. "Can you feel your legs?"

I wiggle one. Then the other.

"Does that mean they're not broken?" Dakota asks. She wipes her eyes with the back of her hand. Mud smears her cheeks.

Hank doesn't answer. He keeps staring at me. "You're lucky you had jeans on. Try moving your arms."

I do. My elbows are killing me. Blood trickles down my arms and mixes with sawdust and dirt.

Dakota touches my shoulder. I feel her trembling.

Hank shakes his head. "You just about gave me a heart attack."

"Sorry," I say.

"I think we should get you inside." He slides his arms under me.

Dakota gets to her feet. "Hank, are you sure it's okay to move her?"

Again, Hank ignores her and talks to me. "Let me know if anything hurts too much. Okay?"

I nod. When I do, my hair—my wig—slides to the ground. Dakota picks it up, shakes it out, and sticks it back on. She doesn't look at me when she does it. They've seen me without my wig before, but I can tell we all feel weird about it anyway. Hank acts like he doesn't see. Chemo doesn't turn everybody bald, but it did me.

Hank picks me up like I'm a feather.

"I can walk, Hank." My voice comes out a whisper. Not real convincing.

"Am I carrying you?" Hank asks, striding out of the barn. "You're so light, I wasn't sure."

Hank's kidding, but he's not that far off. My kind of cancer messes with my stomach and appetite. I'll be starting junior high next week, but I still have to shop for clothes in the girls' department.

Hank hollers over his shoulder, "Dakota, will you put the last horse in the pasture? Give them all grain. And hay for the ones in the barn."

"No problem," Dakota says, jogging back to the trailer.

I wanted to help them with the horses.

Instead, as usual, I've made things harder on everybody.

"Kat!" Dad barrels out of the house and runs at us, faster than I've ever seen him move. "Kat! Kat!" he screams.

"Tell him I'm okay." I know I can't yell loud enough.

"Dad, she's okay!" Hank shouts. "She didn't faint. She just fell in the barn." He adds under his breath, "And was dragged a few yards."

I elbow him. It hurts. Me, not him.

Dad lumbers up to us. He's panting so hard that I'm afraid he'll have a heart attack. Dad's a head shorter than Hank and probably 50 pounds heavier. "What happened? How did she fall? I should have been there." He glances up at the sky and mutters, "Father, thank You for being there." Then he looks at me, and his eyes double in size. "Your arm!"

Maybe I look worse than I thought. I've never seen Dad this upset. Not even when I had that bad reaction to a new medicine. Not even when I threw up all over him in the Nice grocery store the first week I moved here.

"Dad, I'm okay. Really."

"She can move her arms and legs," Hank

says. He starts walking toward the house again.

"But what happened? How did you fall? Where'd you fall from? Does your head hurt?" Dad's short legs shuffle alongside us. He reaches out like he wants to carry me himself.

"Dad, I've got her," Hank says, stopping at the house. "Could you get the door?"

"Of course. Yes. The door." Dad fumbles with the latch. It takes him three tries to get the screen open for us.

"It looks worse than it is," I tell him. "My elbows are scraped."

Two of Wes's rescued dogs slip outside when we come in. Mustard and Ketchup, two of my rescued cats, sneak inside with us.

"Take her upstairs," Dad says. "I'll call my Annie."

"Don't call Mom," I beg over Hank's shoulder, as he takes the stairs two at a time with me. "I'll be fine until she gets home from the hospital."

But Dad's already disappeared into the kitchen to call her.

My mom is an oncologist, a cancer doctor at Nice Hospital. That's where I saw her for the first time. I was only seven, but I was already collecting firsts. The social worker brought me in for my first radiation treatment. "This is Dr. Annie Coolidge," she said. I remember thinking that I'd never seen hair that curly. She was short and stout, and she kept losing her pencil. She didn't look anything like a doctor, but I trusted her from the first minute I saw her.

Hank shoves open my bedroom door and lays me down on the bed, on top of my cat bedspread. "What should I get you? Want some water? Should I turn on your fan?"

I think about asking him to take me off the spread so I don't get it dirty, but it's too late anyway. "I'm okay. Thanks, Hank."

Kitten hops onto the bed and curls up beside me. Her purring motor starts right up.

Dad's voice rises with the sound of his heavy footsteps on the stairs. "Now, now, my Annie. We can keep Kat comfortable until . . . Of course. . . . I promise. . . . Darling, I said I promise."

Still holding the phone to his ear, Dad stumbles into my room. "I'm here with her right now. Hank's taking good care of her and . . . Well, yes, if you want, but . . ." He glances at me. "Your mother would like to talk to you."

"Sure." I reach for the phone. "Ouch!" My elbow stings. Dad puts the phone to my ear.

"Kat? Are you okay? Your head. Did you hit your head?" Mom sounds panicked. "What hurts?"

"Mom, I'm okay. Really. I scraped my elbows. It was a stupid accident."

"I'm leaving the hospital right now. Getting into the van." I hear the door open. The alarm goes off. "Oh, dear. What did I do?"

I turn to Dad. "Mom set off the alarm again. You better take it."

Dad takes back the phone and walks Mom through the steps to disarm the alarm system. They were made for each other. I've been with Dad when *he* had to call Mom to walk him through this same process.

Dad and Hank do their best to clean up my face and arms. But they're so afraid of hurting me that they quit the second Dakota joins us.

"Horses are all pastured, stabled, and fed," Dakota says.

"Thanks, Dakota. Here," Hank says, tossing her his washcloth. "You take over."

"Me?" Dakota catches the rag and acts like it's poison.

"Good idea," Dad agrees. He sets down his bowl and washcloth and kisses my forehead. "Dakota can help you get out of those jeans. Your mother should be here in a little while. She'll know what to do. Are you sure you're not in pain? Are you telling us everything, Kat? Because you—"

"My arms hurt. My hands burn. My knees don't feel so good. But I'm okay, Dad."

Hank and Dad close the door after them, and Dakota gets out a nightgown. It takes us 11 minutes to get me into it. I know because I have a cat-shaped clock on my wall next to my cat calendar.

When we're done, I lie down again, and Dakota sits on the bed with me. She picks up my wig from the floor, where I guess it fell during my struggle with the nightgown.

"Just put it on the bedpost," I tell her. I've never been able to sleep in the thing.

Dakota sets my wig on the bedpost at the foot of my bed and straightens the long blonde hairs. She looks like she's the one who was dragged behind a horse. Her face is streaked with dirt, and her black hair springs around her head in long, wet clumps.

"I can't believe your legs aren't more banged up," she says. "Your knee's purple, though. That's got to hurt." She touches my right knee.

"Ow!" My whole leg throbs with pain.

"I'm sorry!" Dakota cries, scooting away.

"That's okay. Guess I banged it up pretty good."

"You could have been killed."

My mind flashes back to the barn, to the moment when I thought I was going to die. I wasn't ready. I didn't want to die. Not because I'm scared of dying. I don't think I am. How can I be scared of being in a place where I can talk to God without other things getting in the way? Whatever heaven's like, I know it's better than here. And here is pretty great.

But I know I'm not ready because I haven't done anything with my life. That's what I learned in that barn today. I need to do something with my life, like Mom and Dad and Hank do all the time. And I need to do it now.

Knock! Knock!

"Kat! Can I come in?" Dad calls through the door.

"Come in," I holler back.

He bursts in, waving an envelope. Mustard and Ketchup prance into the room behind him. They don't jump up on my bed, not with Kitten there.

"Look what came in the—" He stops when his gaze reaches my knees. "Your knee is purple." He walks closer. "I can't stand thinking about how much that must hurt." His eyes fill with tears.

"It's not so bad," I say quickly. "You know I bruise easily." That part's true. I think it's because of one of the meds I'm on.

A horn honks outside. Brakes squeal.

"Sounds like Mom's home," I say.

Dad runs outside to meet her. In seconds they're racing up the stairs.

Dakota moves out of the way.

Mom rushes to my bed. "Kat, Kat, Kat," she mutters, kissing my forehead and cheeks.

"I'm okay," I manage.

"We'll just see about that." She turns to Dad and Dakota. "Everybody out."

Mom shoos them from my room, then

transforms from mother into Dr. Coolidge, oncologist. She opens her doctor's bag and, for the next 17 minutes, by the cat clock, examines me head to toe.

When she's done, she sits on the foot of my bed and drops her head into her hands. I know she's praying. I just hope it's a thank-You-God prayer and not a how-could-You-let-Kat-be-in-such-bad-shape prayer.

When she looks up, her eyes are red. "God had you in His palm, Kat," she says quietly.

I grin. I'm thinking of that psalm that talks about stumbling but not falling because God holds your hand. I've always pictured a parent holding a little kid's hand and not letting go when the kid's feet fly out from under him.

"You know I've never been all that fond of horses," Mom says.

Mom loves all animals, just like the rest of us. She can't stand to see one suffering or homeless. She patches up cats, dogs, and horses if the vet can't get here in time. She even brought home a bird with a broken wing once and nursed it back to health.

"When I think of what could have happened to you . . ." Her voice trails off.

I put my hand on her arm. She's wrapped my right hand in bandages so it looks like I'm a one-gloved boxer. "I'm okay, right?"

She sighs. "Nothing's broken," she admits.

Footsteps thunder up the stairs.

"Come on in," Mom hollers.

Dad enters, and I catch the look he and Mom exchange, full of meaning, like only they can pull off. I think Dad's asking if I'm really okay and Mom's saying I am but she was really scared, and now she's just thanking God it wasn't worse and Dad's agreeing with her. But they don't say anything out loud, and the look lasts only a couple of seconds, by the cat clock.

Then Dad waves his envelope over his head and shouts, "It came!"

"It came?" Mom jumps up from the bed and reaches for the envelope. She opens it and looks inside. "Where's the letter?"

"Not there?" Dad peeks in for himself. "I must have left it downstairs."

"Left what downstairs?" I ask.

"I'll go down and get it." Dad turns to leave.

"Don't you dare!" Mom says. "Chester

Coolidge, you come back here right this minute and tell me what they said."

"Two weeks from Saturday," he declares.

Mom grabs him and dances him around the room.

They're making even less sense than usual. Maybe I did hit my head after all.

Dakota and Hank appear in the doorway.

"What's going on?" Dakota demands.

"Two weeks!" Dad answers.

"Two weeks?" Hank glances at me, and I shrug.

"Kat's adoption . . . ," Mom begins.

". . . will be final in two weeks!" Dad finishes.

Hank lets out a whoop.

Dad grabs Mom for another dance around the room.

Dakota runs up to high-five me but stops when she sees the bandages on my hand.

I want to whoop or dance or high-five too. But something won't let me. And it's not the bandages.

Ever since I became a foster child of Annie and Chester Coolidge, I've dreamed of the day I'd be adopted, officially, by them. They're so good. They help everybody. Mom saves lives at the hospital. Dad saves lives working for the fire department.

And now *I'm* about to be a Coolidge too.

But I haven't done anything.

THREE

"KAT COOLIDGE," Dakota says, grinning at me. "Katharine Coolidge. Has a nice ring to it."

I try to return her grin. But all I can think is that now I have only two weeks to do something that could make me worth calling myself a Coolidge. I can't become a doctor or join the fire department. Even Wes has turned into somebody people need. The old people at the assisted-living home couldn't get along without the dogs he's trained for them.

I know I can't train horses like Hank and Dakota. But there should be something I can do, some way to help. Maybe if I had another chance with that pony . . .

"Kat?" Mom touches my forehead with the back of her hand. "Honey, are you feeling okay? You're so quiet."

"I'm fine. I guess I'm just tired."

Dad walks up behind Mom and puts his arm around her. "Say, maybe this will help. Kat, what's a cat's favorite song?"

Mom gives him a fake punch. "Chester Coolidge, one of your jokes will most certainly not help."

Hank and Dakota trip over each other in a rush to get out of the room. Dad's pretty famous for his bad jokes and riddles. But I know how much he loves telling them, so I play along. "I don't know, Dad. What's a cat's favorite song?"

"'Three Blind Mice'!" He barely gets it out before he starts cracking up.

"I didn't hear that!" Dakota shouts from the stairs.

"Time to go now," Mom says, gently pushing Dad toward the door.

He obeys but turns back and shouts, "What's a cat's favorite car?"

"Chester!" Mom cries, shoving him with both arms now.

"What's a cat's favorite car, Dad?" I ask.

Mom has him out the door and out of sight. But I hear him shout, "A CAT-illac! Get it, Kat? Cadillac, *Cat*illac?" His voice fades on the stairs.

I close my eyes. I think it's just for a couple of minutes.

When I open my eyes again, I can feel someone watching me. I look to the door, and Wes is standing there.

Wes has been at Starlight Animal Rescue just over a year. He's small for 14, but when he frowns, like he is now, he looks older. Until a couple of weeks ago, Wes was the angriest person I'd ever met. I know he misses his mother, who's back in Chicago, bouncing between jail and rehab. But God's been working overtime on Wes.

"Hey." My voice is gravelly from all the sawdust I swallowed.

Wes doesn't move from the doorway, but Rex, his German shepherd, trots up to my bed and sticks his nose in my face. Kitten shifts from my pillow to my feet. She's not a big Rex fan. I think the other two cats might be hiding under the bed.

"Good dog, Rex," I say. "Come on in, Wes."

He steps into the room like it's booby-trapped. "They said you were okay. You don't look okay."

I wave my bandaged hand at him. "This is way overkill. Mom says I can take it off tomorrow. I'm just scratched and bruised." I scoot up so I'm sitting in bed. It's tough to get comfortable. "You can come closer."

Rex's tail thumps the floor.

Wes stops a couple of feet from my bed. "Hank never should have let you near the barn."

"I wanted to help."

"Dakota should have known better too," he says, like he hasn't heard me.

Rex barks once. It's a warning. Dad calls Wes's dog his "anger-meter." Rex knows when Wes is getting mad before Wes does.

"It wasn't their fault," I explain. "It was a stupid accident. If I hadn't grabbed the pony's lead rope, I wouldn't have gotten hurt."

"But you did!" Wes snaps. "And look at you now."

Rex barks louder.

Wes opens his mouth like he's going to yell at Rex. Then he presses his lips together and leans down to pet his dog. Rex stops barking. I think we're going to be okay.

"Lucky for you there's a doctor in the house," Wes says. His shoulders relax as he keeps stroking Rex's head. I've read somewhere that animals can lower blood pressure. I'll bet it's true with Wes and Rex.

We're quiet for a minute. Then he asks, "Does it hurt?"

"Only when I laugh."

A closed-lips grin tugs at the corners of his mouth. "I'll tell Popeye to keep his jokes to himself then."

I don't remember when Wes started calling Dad "Popeye." Dad doesn't mind. I think he kind of likes it. Plus, it fits. He's bald, stocky, strong, and pretty much a hero.

"Tell me what's going on at the nursing home," I beg.

Wes comes to life. "You should see Munch. I admit that dog won't win any beauty contests, but Miss Golf brings her in to work with her, and Munch can push Buddy's wheelchair now! Bag barks at Rose when her phone's ringing and she can't hear it. And little Moxie's learned to pick up books and pens and things when people drop them." He keeps going with stories from Nice Manor, filled with characters like Leon and Buddy and Moxie and Munch.

I guess I must have slipped off to sleep because all of a sudden Wes is tiptoeing out of my room. "Sorry, Wes," I say, yawning.

"Go back to sleep. You need it. I'll bring you dinner later if you're hungry." He shuts the door after him, leaving me alone with Kitten stretched across my waist like a fuzzy belt.

* * *

The next time I open my eyes, it's dark. Through the window, dozens of stars twinkle, including most of Orion and half of the Big Dipper.

I click on the lamp beside my bed and see that Mustard and Ketchup have made themselves at home on my bed, a safe distance from Kitten. Mustard is an overweight tabby I rescued from the Nice Animal Shelter. Ketchup is a sweet gray longhair I found in a ditch out front. I think the cat had been hit by a car.

She was so bloody that I thought she was red. That's why I named her Ketchup.

I need to find homes for Mustard and Ketchup, but I've been holding out for an owner who will take both of them. House rule is that I can't rescue more cats until I find homes for these. Kitten's different. Mom agreed I could keep Kitten forever.

I sit on the edge of my bed a minute before heading to the bathroom. When I stand, I'm a little dizzy. And when I walk, every part of me aches. I wonder if this is what Gram Coolidge feels like when her arthritis acts up.

"Kat!" Dakota runs into my room and puts her arm around my waist. "You should have called me. I tried to stay awake."

"I'm okay. Just stiff. Thanks." She walks me to the bathroom. "I can take it from here, Dakota."

"You sure you're all right?" she asks. I nod. "Then I'll go down and get you something to eat. You missed dinner. All they could talk about was your adoption being final. Are you hungry?"

I shrug. "I'm kinda thirsty."

"I'll bring something up."

When I come out of the bathroom, Dakota's already back with a sandwich, milk, and cookies. It's 2:17 a.m. by the cat clock.

I sit on the bed and drink half of the milk in one gulp. "Thanks, Dakota. You can go back to bed."

She sets the sandwich and cookies on my dresser. "Are you sure you're okay? I could get Annie."

"I'm okay," I tell her. "I'll finish the milk and go back to sleep."

"If you're sure," she says, yawning.

I do try to fall asleep. Only I can't. I keep thinking about my adoption being final in two weeks. That's not very long. Not if I want to do something to prove to myself that I belong in this family.

I roll over, scooting Kitten off my pillow. When I close my eyes, I see the spotted horse with scabs and scars on her flank, the gray mare with her ribs sticking out, that scared-looking sorrel. And the chestnut pony. I try to imagine how he got that limp. Or the long scar on his head.

I wish I knew more about horses. Understanding cats has always come naturally to me. I'm not as great with them as Hank's cousin Catman. But Catman's taught me a lot through our e-mails.

Suddenly, more than anything, I want to e-mail Catman Coolidge. I'm not sure why I think he'll understand. Hank calls his cousin "a man of few words," and Dad agrees. But in our e-mails, Catman has a way of saying just the right thing.

I say a quick prayer for super strength and stand up again. Mustard and Ketchup stay where they are, on the foot of my bed. Kitten curls around my feet, ready to follow. Taking a deep breath, I start the long trek downstairs to the computer.

My knees feel a stab of pain with every stair step, but the thought of writing Catman makes it worth it.

Sometimes when I can't sleep, I come downstairs and sit in the dark and soak up what I call the "Coolidgeness" of our home. I love the smell of the living room. When Dakota first moved in, she said the house smelled like rain. She meant it as a slam, but I love that smell. It's what I imagine most grandmas' houses smell like.

I never met my biological grandmother.

My bio mom gave me up when I was four. Every time I try to remember what she looked like, all I come up with are her eyes. Her eyes were tired. Tired and sad. I can almost picture her lying on an orange couch, her back to me. I think she's crying, but I don't understand why. She's wearing an orange nightgown or maybe an orange T-shirt. I see my hand reaching up to touch her shoulder, but she shakes it off. She has a cigarette between two fingers, the tip orange, like her gown.

I hope she's quit smoking.

Without meaning to, I reach for the two scars on the inside of my left arm. They're rough and soft at the same time, like tiny stones the ocean hasn't finished smoothing yet. My old doctor, the one I had before I met Mom, told us they were scars from a cigarette.

But they're not. I think I'd remember a thing like that.

I'm not sure how long I've been standing at the foot of the stairs, staring into the darkness. Kitten rubs against my bare legs like she's on duty. Back and forth, back and forth. I pick her up and turn on the light. "Come on, Kitten," I whisper. "Let's write Catman."

I pour myself another glass of milk, then settle in at the computer. The screen sits on the little desk between the kitchen and living room. Mom and Dad like to keep an eye on where we go on the Internet. The screen saver flashes pictures while I drink my milk: Dakota on her horse, Blackfire. Hank riding Starlight, the first animal rescued here. Hank's horse is blind, but you'd never guess it if you saw them galloping down the road together, like they are in this picture.

Wes and Rex come up next. Wes is holding his hand in front of his face, but he wasn't quite quick enough to get out of the picture. His fingers are calloused and dark—Wes is African American—and they stretch across his whole face, like he's about to change masks.

Then the old photos cycle in, and my favorite one of all time comes on the screen. It's a picture of Hank and Catman in front of Gram Coolidge's roses. They can't be more than six or seven years old, and even then you could tell how different they are. It's not just that Hank has dark hair and Catman's is long and blond. Hank's standing straight, focused on the camera. You get the feeling that he's just mowed the lawn, organized the garage, and walked a dozen old ladies across the street. On the ground in front of Hank sits Catman, cross-legged, his right hand raised in a peace sign. And on his lap is a big black cat.

I move the mouse to wake up the computer. In a few seconds, I'm logging on to my e-mail with one hand. I'm a hunt-and-peck, two-finger typer anyway.

While I wait for my in-box to fill, my thoughts start running wild again. In two weeks I'm supposed to go before a judge and declare that I want to be a Coolidge forever. Ms. Bean, my social worker, explained it all to me. It's like a marriage, where we all get one last chance to say "I do."

I do. Of course, *I* do. Who wouldn't want to be the daughter of Annie and Chester Coolidge?

But what about them?

Why would they want someone like me to have their name? The name of Hank Coolidge. Catman Coolidge. They deserve the name *Coolidge*.

But me?

My spam filter kicks in and snaps up most

of the messages heading for my in-box. A few pieces of junk get through. Then I see I've got an e-mail from Catman. I go straight to it.

Hey, Cool Kat!

Man, I dig your last list of firsts. Three cats purring in sync? Groovy, Kat!

Far out, seeing Uncle Chester petting Kitten for the first time. That cat's coming around. So's Kitten. (You dig?)

Standing by for more Kat firsts. Lay 'em on me, man!

Stay cool,

The Catman

It feels better, imagining Catman at the other end of cyberspace. Since Catman graduated from high school last year, he's been on the road, off and on, filming his "cat-umentary" on cats in rural America. But he's never failed to answer my e-mails. I hit Reply and type back:

Dear Catman,

Thanks for writing. You have no idea how much I needed to find you here. Kind of like one of the prayers I didn't even ask and God answered it anyway.

It's been quite a day. But I do have a lot of firsts to report.

I sit back in the chair. Typing with one hand is taking me longer than I thought it would. Plus, I'm feeling a little sick to my stomach, the way I feel a lot of mornings. I wanted to type a big list of firsts I've been keeping in my head for the Catman. But I'm not sure how long I can stay up.

I cut to the chase.

Kat's Firsts for Today:

* Today I rode a pony for the first time. Only thing is, I always thought my first horse ride would actually be ON the horse.

I stop typing and stare at the screen so long that it powers down. My mind is powering down too. I need to get upstairs and back to bed.

I maneuver the mouse and hit Send.

For a minute, I stay where I am, gathering courage to tackle the stairs again. Going up is bound to be harder than coming down.

The computer slips into screen saver mode, triggering the slide show of photos back into action. The first picture that comes up is of me. I'm sitting on the lowest branch of the big oak tree out front. I look like a ghost. Pale face, my long blonde wig uncombed, white shorts and white T-shirt.

Just sitting there. Like now.

Just sitting there. Not doing a thing for anybody.

Just sitting there. Not looking anything at all like a real Coolidge.

Four

The rest of the night is filled with fitful dreams and flashes of sleep. Each time I wake up, there's a second of panic before I make myself think of that psalm and picture God holding my hand. Then I drift back to sleep until it happens all over again.

A couple of times I sense people checking in on me. But it's too hard to open my eyes.

It's totally bright and sunshiny before I drag myself out of bed. Even the cats have bailed on me.

"You're up at last." Mom shuffles into my room in lime green tights and an oversize plaid shirt that fits snug around her middle. She's still wearing her fuzzy red bedroom slippers.

"You look Christmassy," I say, yawning in the general direction of her slippers.

"Do I?" She sounds pleased.

I squint at the cat clock and can't believe the cat's paws are at two again, only it's two in the afternoon this time.

"Feeling any better?" Mom asks, hovering over me. "You need to get fluids in you, Kat."

"My little Kat." Dad rushes in and kisses the top of my head. I feel it, which means I don't have my wig on. "One day closer to your adoption being final," Dad announces. "Hungry? Which reminds me ... Do you know what cats eat for breakfast?"

Mom elbows him, but she's laughing already.

"What *do* cats eat for breakfast, Dad?" I ask.

"*Mice* Krispies! Get it?" He laughs so hard that he breaks into a coughing fit.

Mom slaps him on the back until he's back to normal. "Come on. We'll help Kat downstairs."

"You guys go ahead. I can get downstairs on my own."

"Don't we know it," Dad says.

Mom explains, "Your father played detective this morning. He deduced that you got up in the wee hours, drank some milk, and read your e-mail."

"Not bad," I admit.

"You have five new e-mails from Catman, by the way," Dad says.

"Catman's mother called this morning to make sure you were all right. We filled them in on your accident." Mom pulls a curler out of her hair, letting the curl bounce across her forehead. "Your aunt Claire is quite a character. She was so upset I could hardly understand her. Bart had to take the phone from her. He said Catman had heard from you last night and was really worried."

"You think Claire's a character?" Dad laughs. "My little brother, Bart—now *there's* a character for you." Dad's only a few minutes older than his twin, but he still calls Bart his little brother. Whenever Dad talks about him, his eyes get big like his head's filling with memories. "That man tells the corniest jokes. Always has."

"I'm sure he learned everything he knows from his big brother," Mom says, hugging him from behind. Her arms don't reach around.

"Do you get to stay home today, Dad?" I ask, pulling on my wig.

"No! What time is it?" He squints at my cat clock. "Oh my. I better get going or I'll be late to the firehouse." He comes over and kisses my cheek. "You sure you'll be okay, Kat?"

I nod. "Thanks, Dad. I'm good."

"Great. Then I'm off to the firehouse. Can't wait to tell the guys the good news! In two weeks, Kat will officially join the long and distinguished line of Coolidges." He takes Mom's hand. "Walk me to the car, my Annie?"

Mom leaves with Dad. By the time I get myself cleaned up and dressed, I feel like going back to bed.

"Hey, Kat," Dakota calls when I finally make it downstairs. "I was just heading out to the barn." She has one hand on the screen door. Dogs and cats circle her feet, waiting for their chance to bolt.

"Hang on, Dakota." I make my way toward her and try not to walk like a robot. "I wanted to ask you something about that pony."

She lets go of the screen and meets me half-way. "I know. I'm sorry about that crazy animal. I never should have let you near that pony."

"No. I wanted to help. It wasn't your fault. Or his. That's what I wanted to talk to you about. Do you think I could help with him? I know I could handle him."

Dakota lets out a sharp laugh that's not really a laugh at all. "You're kidding, right? You want to *handle* the pony that dragged you across the barn?"

"That won't happen again."

"You bet it won't. You're not getting near that horse, Kat." Dakota's brown eyes narrow to dark slits.

Hank walks in. "What's going on?"

"Hank, make her listen," I plead. "Yesterday wasn't that pony's fault."

He turns to Dakota. "Kat's right. I think the chestnut's pretty good-natured from what I can see."

"Me too." I'm relieved to have an ally.

"Fine," Dakota says. "The chestnut is a peach of a pony. Kat's still not riding it."

"What?" Hank wheels on me. "You want to ride that horse?"

"I didn't say that." But I *would* love to ride him. "I just want to help with the pony. Is it so crazy to think I might be able to help you guys?"

"Yeah. It's crazy," Dakota says.

I take a deep breath and try again in a calmer voice. "Isn't there anything I can do?" I stare into Hank's blue eyes, counting on the fact that he has trouble saying no to people.

Hank tilts his head toward Dakota. "We do have our hands full."

"I don't believe this." She sounds disgusted. "If you need me, I'll be in the barn." Wes's three-legged Pomeranian slips out behind her before the screen door slams.

I grin at Hank. "I'll do anything, Hank. I just want to help. And I promise I won't do anything stupid like grabbing that lead rope."

But Hank's not looking at me. He's staring over my head.

I turn to see Mom standing there. She's frowning like she's overheard everything.

"Mom, I didn't know you were still here," I admit.

"I noticed," she answers.

"I'm not asking to work with the horses

or ride them. I just want to help." I think about trying to explain to her why this is so important to me. But I'm not even sure I understand it myself. I know it's tied up with becoming a real Coolidge. But I can't say that.

Hank speaks up first. "That chestnut pony is lame. We're going to have to keep him in the stall for a few days at least. Kat wouldn't have to set foot in the pasture."

I could hug Hank for being on my side.

"Hank," Mom says, "Kat wasn't in the pasture yesterday, was she? When that horse dragged her around the barn? There's plenty of room to get hurt in a stall."

"But I won't—"

Hank cuts me off. "Then she'll stay out of the stalls, too," he says.

"Hank!" I protest. "If I can't even get near the pony, how am I supposed to help him?"

"Well," Mom says, completely ignoring me, "I suppose if she doesn't get in the stalls, she'll be safe."

"I'll keep her out of the stall," Hank promises.

"Hello? I'm right here. What can I do without getting into the stall?"

Hank grins. "You can give the pony his medicine, Kat. The vet says we have to give the Butazolodine twice a day. With everything else I've got to do around here, plus the extra horses, not to mention the fact that school starts Monday, I don't need another chore. If you can take over this one, it would be one less thing I'd have to do."

"Really, Hank?" I'm trying to read him. "You're not just making this up so I'll feel better?"

His forehead wrinkles exactly like Dad's does when he's paying bills. "Making what up? The horse needs meds. I hate that job. And I'm too busy to add one more thing."

"And you *promise* Kat won't get inside the stall with that horse?" Mom demands.

"She'll just bute the pony in his feed twice a day so I won't have to," Hank explains.

"Please, Mom?" I beg.

Mom walks up to me and starts unwrapping the bandages from my hand. "Do you promise to keep a stall between you and that horse?"

"Promise."

"Okay," Mom finally agrees.

I hug her. Then I hug Hank. "When do I start?"

"No time like the present," Hank says. "You up for it?"

Truth is, all I'm up for is going back to bed. But I'm not about to tell them that. "Lead on."

"HANK?" He's halfway to the barn before I can even clear the front porch.

"Sorry, Kat." Hank jogs back. He sticks out his arm, and I take hold. His arms are thicker than my legs. "I've been trying to figure out what to do with the old sorrel. She's been used up on the trails. I'd love to let her pasture with some yearlings. She's got great manners in spite of everything. That gray mare is still a mystery to me. Not sure what's going on with her. And the Pinto's so scared that I'll probably have to imprint her, start her all over again like a colt."

I like that he's talking to me about the horses as if we're in this together. "If anybody can help these horses, Hank, it's you. Or Winnie, of course."

Hank grins. "Of course. Did I tell you Uncle Bart and Aunt Claire and Catman might come out here for Thanksgiving?"

"That would be great!"

"Yeah. Gram goes there every Thanksgiving. It's time for them to come up here. Catman always acts like his cats couldn't get along for a few days without him."

"You're the same way with your horses, and you know it," I say.

We reach the barn. Seeing the sawdust brings back everything that happened yesterday. I look away and follow Hank to the tack room.

"I'll show you where I keep the meds," Hank says. "You can dump feed into the pony's trough from the stallway."

"I wish I could do more," I say, half to myself.

"I'm not kidding when I tell you this helps, Kat. It's a hassle to remember to give a horse medicine. I'll be too busy with the other horses.

The faster I get them fattened up and gentled again, the better chance we'll have of finding good homes for them. It's going to be tougher once school starts too."

The tack room is about the size of my bedroom. Feed bins line one wall. Bridles hang on the opposite wall. A bunch of different kinds of saddles are stacked up on sawhorses. Gram Coolidge is always bringing over tack she's picked up at an auction or at a barn sale.

Hank lifts the lid on a wooden box that's sitting in the far corner. "You don't have to refrigerate bute. Just keep it in here with the syringes."

Syringes? "This stuff comes in pills, right? No shots?"

Hank laughs. "No shots." He pulls out a large white envelope and shakes a giant pill into his palm.

I can't believe how big the pill is. Bigger than a quarter and three times as thick. "Hank, how can you expect that poor little pony to swallow *that*?"

He bites his lip like he's trying not to laugh. "We'll crush it up first, Kat."

"Crush it up," I repeat. "Good call."

He glances around the tack room, spots an empty coffee can, and sets it on the old school desk Gram Coolidge found last fall at a garage sale. "You can crush it up in this." He hands me the pill and the can, then stands back.

I try to break the pill in half. It won't break.

Hank takes the pill back. He gets a pair of pliers from the toolbox. Then he holds the pill over the coffee can. "This will be easier for you. Pinch off pieces all the way around, like this."

Snip, snip, snip. Pieces of the pill drop into the coffee can. "There." He sets the pliers down. "You can do the other pill. Two pills in the morning. Two in the evening. Got it?"

I stare at the white, chalky dust in the bottom of the can. "Won't it taste horrible?"

"I never tried one, but it probably does," Hank admits. "Which is why you mix it with oats. Okay?" He nods and starts to leave.

"How much oats?" I know I'm bugging him with too many questions. But I don't want to do it wrong.

Hank's about as patient as they come, but he sighs. "Two of the scoops, Kat. They're in the green bin with the oats. And leave the scoop in the bin when you're done. Okay?"

"Okay. Thanks."

Hank heads for the door, but he turns back. "Second thoughts?"

"Not on your life, cowboy." I pick up the pliers and wave good-bye to him.

Once he's gone, I shake out the second pill. I position the pliers just like Hank did, hold the pill over the can, and squeeze.

Nothing happens.

I try again. I squeeze harder. And harder. My hand aches. My shoulder hurts.

"I can do this," I mutter. I use both hands and every bit of muscle.

Dakota sticks her head into the tack room. She's got her horse, Blackfire, by the reins. "Everything okay in here?"

"Great. Thanks, Dakota."

She doesn't look like she buys it, but she leaves.

This is ridiculous. I try everything, including beating the stupid white pill with the pliers. It doesn't even crack.

How can I be so useless? I can't even break a pill.

God, I don't suppose You'd like to have lightning strike this pill? Or a tiny earthquake, maybe?

Nothing happens.

Didn't think so.

Then I get an idea. Hank has hammers hanging on the wall, neatly organized by size. I pull one down and raise it over the pill. "Great idea, Kat," I mutter, "if you really want to splatter medicine all over the tack room."

But if I had a plastic bag . . .

I check to make sure Dakota and Hank are in the pasture. Then I make my way to the house and get a box of plastic sandwich bags. Back in the tack room, I drop the evil pill into the bag, sealing it and then double-bagging it to be safe.

"Here goes." I lift the hammer with both hands and bring it crashing down on the pill. It breaks into several pieces, all of them staying inside the bag. "Gotcha!" I exclaim.

A few more well-placed whacks, and that pill is dust. I empty the bag into the coffee can with the pill Hank crushed. Then I dump in oats and shake it up. The white powder blends in with the oats, making it look like cookie mix before you put the butter in. The whole thing smells too familiar. Not like cookie dough, though. More like the hospital. I sure hope horses don't have a great sense of smell.

Holding out my precious bute mixture, I walk to the stalls. When Hank and Dad started Starlight Animal Rescue, they rebuilt the whole barn, designing the stalls so horses could see out as much as possible. The top of the stall-way door is always open so horses can see us coming. The back of the stalls on this side of the barn open into the pasture.

The pony's back stall door is shut on the bottom, but the top is open. Through it, I see Hank cantering Starlight in the pasture, the Paint's tail flowing behind her. Dakota and Blackfire are trotting after them, with the gray mare on a lead behind her.

The pony is standing alone and silent in his stall, his neck so low his nose almost touches the straw bedding. I want to go in and put my arms around his neck. But I won't.

"We have to get you well so you can play with the other horses, Pony. And I can't keep calling you Pony, either. You need a name."

Kitten climbs the gate, then pounces on

my shoulders. She rubs her face against my cheek and purrs.

"I love you too, Kitten. Help me think of a name for this skinny pony." It hurts to see his ribs poking out from his dull coat. I know there's a beautiful chestnut under that dusty brown. "Chestnut." I roll the name around in my mouth. "What do you think, Kitten?"

Kitten kneads my shoulder with her paws. Her sharp claws hurt a little, but I know she only does it because she loves me.

"It's settled, then. We'll call you Chestnut."

I shake the coffee can to get the powder off the bottom. Chestnut's ears perk forward at the rattle of oats in the can.

I reach in and dump the whole oat mixture into the trough. "Come and get it."

He doesn't.

I step back in case it's me he's afraid of. "Come on, boy."

Chestnut steps cautiously to the trough and lowers his head. His nostrils flare. He lips at the mixture. Then he snorts. White powder flies everywhere. Chestnut jerks up his head and backs away.

"You have to eat it." I try mixing the oats again and hiding the white powder in the trough. It can't be done.

Chestnut stays at the rear of the stall. He won't even try. And I know he's hungry.

"Kitten, I am a complete and total failure." I must have done something wrong, or he would have eaten the oats. I wish I knew more about horses. The last thing I want to do is ask Hank and make him come in from the pasture to do my little job.

"Winnie!" That's it! If anybody in the world could help me with this, it's Winnie the Horse Gentler.

Kitten jumps off my shoulders as I head for the house. My brain's spinning. I could call Winnie. But I don't know her number, and I don't want to ask anybody for it. I could e-mail her. But what if she doesn't check her e-mail for hours? Chestnut needs his medicine now.

Then I remember. It's Saturday. Catman is probably on the road, filming his cat-umentary. But Winnie and Eddy Barker should be at the pet store right now, answering questions on the Pet Helpline. If I hurry, I could still catch Winnie.

SIX

HANK HAS THE PET HELPLINE bookmarked, and it takes me only a few seconds to get there. Postings are going on live, so I jump in:

KoolKat: Sorry to interrupt, everybody. But this is an emergency.

Just like that, a response comes. In seconds, Winnie and I exit the helpline and enter a private chat room:

WinnieTheHorseGentler: Kat! How are you? Catman told us what happened. Your mom said you were okay—but bruised and scraped, right?

KoolKat: I'm fine. Tell Catman I'll write him later. Sorry I left him hanging.

Catman: Chill, Kat. I'm here. All is groovy. So what's the emergency, man?

KoolKat: Great. Okay. Here goes. Chestnut, one of the abused horses Hank rescued, needs Butazolodine. I volunteered to give it to him. I got the pills crushed and mixed with oats. But the pony won't touch it.

Catman: Get my cousin on the case, dude. You shouldn't have to do it.

KoolKat: I want to do it. Hank and Dakota are so busy with the new horses. This is the least I could do . . . and I can't even do this.

WinnieTheHorseGentler: No problem, Kat. Molasses.

KoolKat: Molasses? That sticky stuff that looks like syrup?

WinnieTheHorseGentler: That's the one. Mix it with the oats and bute. Chestnut will eat it.

KoolKat: Winnie, thanks! I knew you'd know what to do.

It takes me a few minutes to find the jar of
molasses behind the cereal boxes. My head is
buzzing, so I know I'm overdoing it. But I can't
stop now. I race to the barn, holding the jar up
in front of me like it's the Olympic torch.

Dakota and Hank are still out in the pasture with the horses. Chestnut's feed trough
is just like I left it. It's a wooden trough, long
enough to hold a salt block and grain.

"You just wait, Chestnut," I tell him. He
sniffs the air while I dump in a glob of molasses.
"You're going to love this. Winnie promised."
There's nothing to stir with, so I use my fingers and mix the powdery oats with the sticky
molasses. "This feels pretty gross," I admit, "but
the smell's not bad."

When it's all mixed, I stand over the
trough and bow my head. My fingers are sticky
and disgusting. "Father, Chestnut and I thank
You for this delicious food before us. Please use
it to make Chestnut well again. Amen."

I look up at Chestnut. His ears rotate back, then forward. His nostrils twitch like a rabbit's. "Come on, boy. You know you want it."

He's not going for it. The memory of the awful white powder must be too fresh in his mind. Hank told me once that horses put elephants to shame when it comes to good memories. An old mare could be frightened her whole life because of something that happened when she was a filly.

Chestnut hovers by the stall door, refusing to take a single step toward the trough. I have to wonder what's happened to this poor pony to make him so cautious.

"Please trust me, Chestnut," I whisper. I dig my hand into the sticky, gooey mixture and come up with a handful of gunk. Then I start singing: "'Amazing grace . . .'" I keep it soft. I'm a pretty bad singer. With my arm out straight, I edge toward the stall door.

Chestnut watches as I stick my hand into the stall. My elbow aches, but I keep my arm stiff and my hand flat. Hank says it's a bad habit to let a horse eat from your hand, but I see him do it all the time.

Chestnut's ears twitch. Then he takes one step toward me.

"Good, Chestnut," I coo. I'm done with "Amazing Grace," so I make up a song. "Chestnut, the snub-nosed horsey–" he takes a step closer–"had a very shiny nose." Chestnut stretches out his neck as far as he can. "And if you ever saw him–" his lips barely reach my fingertips–"you would ask for one of those." His lips tickle my hand. "All of the other horseys . . ." He nuzzles the molasses mixture, getting most of it into his mouth, until all that's left in my hand is a sticky mess.

"Way to go, Chestnut," I whisper. I ease back to the trough and get another handful. We replay the hand-feeding scene. Then I take a third handful, but I don't go to Chestnut this time. Instead, I stretch my hand over the feed trough and wait.

It takes about five minutes and two songs–"Chestnut galloping in an open field. Jack Frost nipping at his hooves . . ." and "O Chestnut tree, O Chestnut tree, how lovely are your brown eyes . . ."–but he comes around. Finally the pony munches straight from his feed trough.

When the last powdery oat is gone, I feel like I've invented ice cream or duct tape. I could list a dozen firsts, including the first time I've been on the doctoring end of giving meds.

I'm still glowing when I hear a *clip-clop*, *clip-clop* crossing the barn.

Dakota walks in, leading two of the abused geldings. "You still here? Everything okay?"

"Yep. I was just chatting with Chestnut."

She grins. "Chestnut?"

"Like it?" I ask.

"Not bad," she admits.

Hank rides in on the gray mare. "Did that pony get the bute down, Kat?" He dismounts and unbuckles the mare's saddle.

"His name is Chestnut," I explain. "And he downed every last bite of the medicine. But he didn't at first. So I mixed it with molasses."

"Good job," Hank says. He pulls off the heavy Western saddle like it's no heavier than a washcloth. "It's a big help. Thanks."

As I leave the barn, Hank's words stay with me. *Good job. Thanks. Big help.*

Maybe I'll make a good Coolidge after all.

"Okay!" Dad shouts over the clang of silverware around the dinner table. Mom cooked a roast, and it's taking a lot of work to cut it. "Where does a cat go when it loses its tail?"

Wes groans. Dakota looks like she's trying not to smile.

I start to repeat Dad's riddle question for him, but Mom beats me to it. "Chester, sweetheart, where *does* a cat go when it loses its tail?"

Dad sets his knife on his plate. "To the *retail* store! Get it? Re-*tail*?" He's laughing so hard he can barely get the words out. "And what is the cat's favorite color in the retail store?"

"I don't know, my love," Mom says, still laughing hard from the last joke.

"What's the cat's favorite color?" Dad repeats. "*Purrrrrrrr*-ple!"

"Funny," Dakota says, not laughing.

Hank's chuckling, but I'm pretty sure it's got more to do with Mom and Dad than with the joke. They're clinging to each other so they won't fall out of their chairs.

Wes is the only one who's managed to finish his meat, although I caught Lion, his three-legged Pomeranian, snatching a table scrap from him. Wes clears his throat. "All right." He says this like we've all been begging him to say something and he's only now given in. "What's up when you hear '*meow . . . splat . . . woof . . . splat . . . meow . . . splat . . . arf . . . splat*'?"

We're all so shocked that Wes would tell a joke or riddle that nobody speaks. He stares from one person to the next. Wes telling a riddle? Now there's a first for my list. I can't wait to write Catman.

Hank comes to his senses first. "Um . . . okay. What's going on when you hear, well, *that?*"

Wes is quiet for so long I'm afraid he doesn't have a punch line. Then he says, "It's raining cats and dogs."

We howl. Mom and Dad fall into each other's arms. Dakota's eyes have tears, she's laughing so hard.

And then it hits. The nausea. It's like an ocean wave rolling over me while my back's turned. I never saw it coming.

I bite my cheek and hope it passes. But I know better. Already the room wobbles. My head feels like it could float off my body.

I push my chair back and stand. The floor is an ocean, and I'm trying to stand on it. I grab the edge of the table to steady myself.

Hank's watching me. The others are still lost in laughter. Hank whispers across the table, "Kat? Need help?"

I shake my head. The room shakes with it. My forehead breaks into a cold sweat.

I dash to the little bathroom off the kitchen. I'm steadier when I'm moving fast. I make it. Close the bathroom door behind me. Drop to my knees.

And hurl.

Vomit.

Puke.

We have a thousand names for it in my house. I'm never sure if it's the cancer or the medicine or what both have done to my kidneys. But throwing up is as much a part of life around here as riddles.

"Everything okay?" Mom asks through the bathroom door. I'm guessing she's been there all along.

I'm still sitting on the cool tile. "I'm okay." I pull myself up and splash water on my face.

"That's good. I'm sliding a pill, a Zofran, under the door. You holler if you need us or anything." Mom's voice is cheery. I love that she does her best to keep things normal. They all do. They try to keep everything as normal as it can be.

I take the pill. Then I check the mirror before walking back to the table. Strands of my wig are stuck to my forehead. My pupils are huge.

I open the door and step out. My head is light, but I think I'm done being sick. Maybe.

"Hey, Kat," Hank calls. "I was just telling them about the pony. We'll keep him on bute for a week."

Dakota says, "I'm getting pretty close to that gray mare. Don't suppose we could keep all eight of the new horses?"

"I hope you're joking," Mom says. "So, who wants dessert?"

"Mom?" As soon as I talk, they all get quiet. "Would you save my dessert for later? I think I'll go upstairs and set out something to wear to church tomorrow."

"Need any help?" Dad asks. He stands.

"No thanks." I try to hurry to the stairs and out of sight. I know they're all watching me, even though little conversations are springing up. I'm so tired that my bony legs feel like redwood trunks as I drag upstairs.

I walk into my bedroom and am greeted by Mustard and Kitten, who fight over me. I don't think the Zofran's helping my nausea.

Another wave of dizziness slaps me. I dash for the bathroom.

I barf.

Upchuck.

Kneel before the porcelain throne.

Make my white-bowl deposit.

And wish I didn't have to be such a burden.

SEVEN

SUNDAY MORNING I don't wake up until everybody has gone to church. Everybody except Dad. I hear him humming hymns in the kitchen. Poor Dad loves church, and he had to miss it so he could keep an eye on me.

I don't feel like getting out of bed. I roll over and face my window, where a tiny breeze moves the cat curtains. I hear a cardinal. To me, they always sound like they're saying, "Birdie, birdie."

Then I see him, a bright red male on the tree limb outside my window. He's close enough to touch if I were at the ledge. But the most amazing thing is that on the limb directly above the cardinal sits a bluebird. We don't see many bluebirds, and this is the first time I've seen both birds at once. It feels like a gift.

I sit up in bed and try to remember Bible verses about animals. I know there are some great ones. I take my Bible off the bedside table and read a few. They're easy to find because those pages are dog-eared. Psalm 104 is one of my favorites: *"The earth is full of your creatures. . . . You open your hand to feed them, and they are richly satisfied."*

I flip back to Deuteronomy 33:26: *"There is no one like the God of Israel. He rides across the heavens to help you, across the skies in majestic splendor."*

I try to imagine God galloping across the heavens to help me.

Galloping.

"Chestnut!" I slam the Bible shut and jump out of bed. I forgot all about the pony. It must be noon by now, and he won't have been fed yet. He needs that medicine.

I pull jeans on over my nightgown and get downstairs just as Mom walks in with Dakota and Hank, followed by Wes.

Dad greets me, then runs to Mom and hugs her like she's been gone a year instead of a morning.

"Kat, you're up," Mom says.

"Sorry I missed church." I brush past them to get outside. But my shoes aren't by the door. "Dakota, have you seen my shoes?"

"Nope," she answers, heading for the fridge.

There must be two dozen shoes out here on the porch, and none of them are mine. "Where could they be? I know I put my sandals out here yesterday." I toss shoe after shoe, searching.

"Why do you need shoes?" Dad asks.

"Yeah," Mom agrees. "Where are you going?"

"To the barn to feed Chestnut." Frustrated, I give up and slip on an old pair of Dakota's boots. They're a few sizes too big, but I don't care.

"That's okay," Hank says. He takes a long swig of ice water as he stands over the sink, then refills his glass. "I fed Chestnut for you. I had to feed the others anyway."

I stop at the screen door, my back to

everybody. Hank fed Chestnut? "That was my job," I mutter.

"What did you say?" Hank asks.

I don't turn around, but I raise my voice. "It was *my* job to feed and bute Chestnut."

"I'm sorry," Hank says. I hear him coming over to me. "If I'd known you'd be . . . up . . . by now, I wouldn't have fed the pony."

"It only took him, like, two minutes, Kat," Dakota says. "No big deal."

I turn to face them and hope my smile looks less fake than it feels. "You're right. Chestnut shouldn't have to go hungry because I slept in. He's supposed to get that medicine the same time every day. That's the way it is with my meds. So, thanks, Hank."

It's all true. I make so much sense, I almost believe myself.

I excuse myself from Dad's Sunday dinner and go back to bed.

The next time I wake up, it's dark. Outside I hear the faint voices of my family and know it's a moon check. On any given night, any one of us can call for a moon check, and the rest of us have to go along. We sit or lie down under the stars. Dad points out constellations and tells the stories that go with them. Hank's almost as good as Dad at picking out planets and constellations. I call for more moon checks than anybody.

The screen slams downstairs. I hear footsteps coming up, then a tap on my door. Wes steps in with a bottle of water. "You awake, Kat?"

"I'm awake." But for somebody who's slept most of the last 48 hours, I don't feel all that awake.

"Good. Annie said you need to drink." He shoves the cold water bottle at me. "You missed old Mrs. Coolidge."

"Gram was here?" I take a big drink. Maybe too big. "Wes, do you know if Hank fed Chestnut for me tonight?"

Wes shrugs. "Probably. I was out walking Rex and Lion, but I saw him go to the barn."

"Well, will you ask Hank just to be sure? Make sure Chestnut got his second dose of bute."

"Sure."

"And tell him I'll take care of the pony myself tomorrow. Before school."

"You sure you're ready for school?" Wes asks.

"I'm not missing the first day of junior high," I insist. I motion for Wes to sit on the bed.

He sits on the rug instead. Rex immediately curls next to him and puts his big head in Wes's lap. "Junior high." Wes says it like he doesn't approve. "Nobody has junior high anymore. Hasn't Nice heard about middle schools?"

I shrug. Wes is going to be a freshman.

"You could stay home if you wanted to," Wes says. "*I* sure would if Annie would let me."

Wes had a rough time in school last year. I think Nice Junior High turned out to be a whole different world from the school he went to in Chicago. "Things will be better this year, Wes. *You're* better. And you'll know kids already."

"Which will be such a bonus, since they all loved me so much last year." Wes can't match Dakota in the sarcasm department, but he's got his share of it.

"Okay. Here's what I do. When you walk into school alone, or into a classroom, imagine you're holding God's hand. So you're not really alone, right?"

Wes laughs, almost. "You know you're the only person who can get away with saying stuff like that, don't you?"

"Has Dakota said anything to you about starting school here? She hasn't said anything at all about it to me."

"Me either." Wes gets to his feet. "Except she hasn't let up complaining about Hank being a junior and her being a sophomore when they're the same age."

They were both born on July 4, 16 years ago, in totally different worlds. "At least they're in the same building. Hank can be there for backup."

"When he's not fending off girls who throw themselves at him," Wes says.

"True." I start to laugh. Only here it comes again, that wave. It hits my head and moves to my stomach.

I press my hand to my mouth and race to the bathroom, making it just in time. There's not much in me, but it all comes out anyway. I heave until my sides ache.

When I walk out of the bathroom, Wes is standing there, studying his shoelaces. "Honking."

I wipe my mouth with the back of my hand. "What?"

"Honking. That's what they call hurling in Scotland."

"Good to know," I say, making my way back to bed. "Don't tell them I *honked* again, okay, Wes? I want them to enjoy the moon check without worrying about me."

He nods. "See you in the morning."

★ ★ ★

In the morning, I'm up by 5:10 on the cat clock. It's a good thing, too. By the time I let out the cats and feed them, then go back upstairs and shower, then get dressed, I hear Mom and Dad having breakfast in the kitchen.

I check myself in the full-length mirror I stash in the corner of my room. I'm not crazy about mirrors, but I need to check out my first-day-of-school outfit. A couple of weeks ago, Gram Coolidge bought me a new shirt and cool tan capris for my first day. Now, sizing myself up in the full-length mirror, I can see that my new clothes are way too big on me.

I change into old jeans that still fit and a

white shirt. Not exactly a fashion statement, but at least I don't look like I'm playing dress-up. And the long sleeves hide my scraped elbows.

I've put on my blonde wig. It's long and straight, but this morning it looks all wrong. I try the short red wig. Too Orphan Annie. I settle on the long black wig and work on the side part.

Before I go downstairs, I have to sit on the bed to catch my breath. I feel like I've already put in a full day.

Kitten weaves between my sandaled feet on every step as I walk downstairs. "Morning, Mom and Dad," I call.

"Kat?" Mom walks to the bottom of the staircase and peers at me. "We thought we heard you getting dressed up there. You look wonderful." She's not as convincing as she probably thinks she is. "I did think you might do better starting later in the week, honey."

Dad joins her. "Nothing much goes on the first day, right?"

My legs are wobbly, so I hurry around them and sit at the table. But the smell of eggs makes something rise in my throat.

"Hey!" Dad shouts, checking something in the oven. "Here's a math question to get you ready for school. Ten cats were in a boat. One jumped overboard. How many were left in the boat?"

I'm afraid to answer. My head's light. I press my lips together to keep everything in.

Mom picks up the slack. "Um . . . how many cats were left in the boat, dear? Wouldn't it be nine?"

"Nope," Dad says, not very heartily. He's sneaking glances at me. "None. They were all copycats."

I get up. "I'm going to the barn." I run outside and honk so hard I think I'll never stop.

EIGHT

I STAY DOUBLED OVER OUTSIDE, leaning against the house until my heart quits racing. The sun is already shining brightly in a clear blue sky. A light breeze rustles the leaves on the trees and cools the morning. Geese fly in a crooked V. A mourning dove's soulful cry comes from behind the barn. It's a perfect, glorious day for my first day of junior high.

Only I won't be there.

I feel Dad's arm slide around my shoulder. "We'll get 'em tomorrow, Tiger Kat."

I let him walk me back to bed. The second I shut my eyes, I'm out.

When I open my eyes, Gram Coolidge is standing over me. She's taller than Dad, with a long face and stylish blonde hair that would look great on somebody my age.

"Good! It's about time." Gram sits on my bed, shoving Kitten off. "Now, I've been working on your birthday party, Kat."

"Gram, I already had my birthday. Remember?" I pull myself up to a sitting position. Nobody should face Gram Coolidge lying down.

"Ah, but this is your Coolidge birthday. We must celebrate your official adoption. I think the best time will be right after you leave the courthouse."

"What courthouse?" I ask. Then I remember what the social worker said about going before a judge to say, "I do." I just didn't picture it all happening in a courthouse.

"The Nice Courthouse, of course," Gram answers. "We can have the party at my house. I'll invite the bridge club. You're welcome to bring any of your little friends, of course."

"Gram, wait." My head is too foggy to keep up with her. My stomach is knotting.

"Too much? Your mother thought you'd

say that. Oh, all right. We'll go to the Made-Rite in town, just like we did for your birthday. Will that do?"

Mom sticks her head into the bedroom. "There you are, George." She's the only person who can call Georgette Coolidge "George." She walks over and takes my pulse. "Need anything before I head to the hospital, Kat?"

"No thanks. I think I'm still sleepy," I admit.

I rest most of the morning, but I can't sleep. I keep imagining what's going on at school without me.

In the afternoon, I make myself eat crackers and drink ginger ale, and I start feeling better again. While I wait for everybody to get home from school, I watch Mustard and Ketchup play with their ball of yarn. They don't play together, just side by side. It reminds me of the way it is at school, where I always seem to be more side by side than *with* anybody. It's not that Nice kids aren't "nice." But sometimes it feels like they're afraid they'll catch cancer from me if they get too close.

By about three o'clock I can't wait any

longer, and I go out to the barn to see Chestnut. Rex tags along. I know he misses Wes.

"Good to see you up, Kat," Dad calls. He's digging a garden on the west side of the house, and he puts down his little shovel.

"Hi, Dad. I'm going to check on Chestnut."

He nods and acts like he's going back to digging. But I can see him peeking at me. He's a terrible pretender, but I appreciate the effort.

Kitten prances toward me when I walk into the barn. Her tail is high, waving slowly. "What are you up to, Kitten?" I ask her. She eyes Rex, who knows enough to keep his distance.

I head for the tack room and pound up two bute tablets, dump them into the coffee can, and mix it with molasses and oats. When I deliver the mix to Chestnut, Kitten is sitting on the pony's back. She's curled up, with her paws under her. I wish I had a camera.

"Hey, Chestnut." I pour the molasses mixture into the feed trough. "Looks like you got yourself a new friend."

Chestnut dives in and cleans his trough.

"Did you see that, Rex?" I bend down to pet the dog's soft head. "I did good." It's crazy to feel this proud about feeding the pony, but I do.

I'm about to go inside when the van drives up. Mom stops under the oak tree, and Wes and Dakota get out. I don't see Hank. And anyway, I thought he took the pickup.

I walk toward the van. "Where's Hank?"

Wes stomps by me. "You'd have to ask Hank. He's too popular to be bothered with us. And I'm not riding with Annie again. I'll tell you that. I'll walk first. Or take the stupid bus." He storms into the house, hollering, "You think I need people seeing me get picked up by my mommy?"

Dakota shrugs. She and Mom and I walk inside together.

Wes has already gone upstairs. Mom pours two glasses of lemonade and heads up after him. Dakota pours herself a big glass of lemonade and collapses onto the couch. I take the other corner of the couch and start pumping her about her day.

"Did you get to know anybody in your classes?" I ask. "Do you have any classes with Alicia?" Alicia and Dakota know each other from church.

"I didn't see her," Dakota answers.

"What about lunch?" I ask. "Who did you eat with?"

"I thought this girl, Charlotte something, was being really cool asking me to sit with her and her friend at their table. She introduced me to everybody. Then she started asking me questions."

"That's good, right?"

"Wrong," Dakota says.

Outside I hear the crunch of gravel. It's probably Hank, but I don't want to get up and look. I think Dakota needs to talk. "What kind of questions did she ask you?"

"Let's see," Dakota begins, and I know this isn't going to be good. "'Are you really Hank's foster sister?' And 'What's Hank really like? What kind of music does he like? Is Hank going out for football? Is he dating anyone?'"

"Ah," I say, understanding why she's so mad. "Sorry, Dakota."

"Yeah. Whatever." She gets up from the couch and starts for the stairs. "Anyway, thanks for listening, Kat. Glad you're feeling better. You were white as a ghost this morning."

Mom comes down the stairs as Dakota

goes up. She kicks off her shoes and collapses in the big chair.

"Did Hank and Wes have a fight?" I ask her.

"No. Not really. Hank was going out with some friends after school, so I said I'd pick up Wes and Dakota. I didn't think about how Wes would feel."

I pull back the curtain and see Hank's truck parked by the barn. But there's no sign of Hank.

Then I get a horrible feeling. What if he's doing chores? What if he feeds Chestnut . . . again?

I dash to the door.

"Kat? What's the matter?" Mom calls.

"Nothing! Be right back." Chestnut's had all the medicine he can have today. Hank can't give him any more. I don't stop running until I'm in the barn, even though my chest heaves and I feel like hurling. "Hank!" I stumble, pick myself up, and stagger to the stallway.

"Kat?" Hank's in front of Chestnut's stall, inches from the feed trough. He's holding the coffee can.

NINE

"**Stop, Hank!**" I scream. "Don't feed Chestnut!" I'm panting so hard I have to bend over to catch my breath.

"Kat? What's wrong with you? Should I get Mom?"

I shake my head. I still can't breathe right, and my voice comes in puffs. "I just . . . had to stop you. You can't feed Chestnut."

"Look," Hank says, "I don't mind. Honest." He shakes the coffee can.

"No!" I cry. I lunge for him and grab for the can. Only I miss. The can sails out of Hank's hands and smashes into his chest, sending oats, bute, and molasses all over the new shirt Gram gave him.

"What's the matter with you?" he shouts. He tries to brush off the sticky mixture, but it smears all over him.

"You can't feed Chestnut . . . because I already did." Tears are coming now, and I can't stop them.

I watch his face as it sinks in. "I almost gave him two more pills," Hank says. "I would have overdosed that pony."

"I know," I whisper. I'm shaking all over.

Hank starts to say something, then stops. He takes a deep breath. I have the feeling he's praying, even though his eyes are wide-open. "Listen, Kat. This could have been bad."

I nod. I know it could have been bad. I can't even think what might have happened if Chestnut had gotten four pills so close together.

Hank is staring into the empty coffee can. I think we're both imagining what could have happened, what almost did happen.

"It's supposed to be my job," I snap.

"I had no way of knowing you already fed Chestnut." His voice is steady–kind even.

And it makes me feel worse. He's right. I'm not mad at Hank. I'm mad at me. What was I thinking? That Hank could read my mind and know when I've fed the horse and when I haven't?

"Maybe we better rethink this."

"No!" I protest. "I can do it!"

"I know. And you did a great job. I've been using your molasses trick. Works like a charm." He's quiet a few seconds, then goes on. "But it's too risky to leave it like this. I don't know how else to handle it. I'm just saying that until you're sure you're better, maybe we shouldn't both be feeding Chestnut the bute. We could get mixed up again."

I start to argue. But he's right. I can't guarantee that I won't be too sick to help. Then what?

Chestnut has to come first.

Tuesday I don't even bother getting dressed until noon. I spend the first hour of daylight hurling into the toilet. Each round feels like I'm being pushed further and further away from becoming a Coolidge, from doing any-thing that would make me worth being a Coolidge.

Mom goes to the hospital, and Dad stays home with me. Nobody's in the house when I finally come downstairs. I check my e-mail and find one from Winnie.

Hi, Kat!

Good to hear the molasses worked for you and Chestnut. And I'm sorry about the problem with the feeding schedules. I've been thinking of another way you could help Hank with the horses, though.

The best thing you can do with horses is watch them. Sounds simple, right? But it's how I learned about horses. My mom and I used to observe mustangs in the wild a long time ago, before she died and Dad moved Lizzy and me to Ohio. Most of what I know about horses I've learned from watching them. Why don't you watch the new horses, Kat? Take notes. Run them by me if you want to. You'll end up helping Dakota and Hank more than you can imagine. How about it? Up for a Kat Horse Clinic?

Love, Winnie

I write her back and thank her. I don't know if I can help the way Winnie thinks I can, but I'm definitely up for trying.

I figure I have at least an hour before everybody gets home from school. Outside, Dad's crouched over the riding lawn mower. Pieces of metal and mower lie scattered in the long grass. "Dad, I'm going to hang out with the horses for a while," I tell him.

His head jerks up. Grease smudges cover his face. "The horses? Is your mother all right with that, Kat?"

"I promise I won't get into the stalls or the pasture. I'm just going to watch."

"That's nice," Dad says, fiddling with the mower again. He pulls out a thin black belt from the overturned engine and acts like he's just delivered a baby. "Ta-da! It's a belt!"

"Congratulations, Dad. I'm off." I head toward the pasture because Hank turned out all the horses except Chestnut this morning.

"Wait! Kat!" Dad calls after me. "Come back!"

I trudge back, ready to do battle if he's changed his mind about letting me hang out with the horses. "What?"

"Why do you always find your cat in the last place you look for him?"

A joke? That's why Dad called me back? I'm so relieved that I feel like laughing. But I'll wait for the punch line. "I don't know, Dad."

"Why do you always find your cat in the last place you look for him? Because after you find him, you stop looking!" Dad and I both laugh so loud that Rex and Lion trot over to see if we're okay.

I leave the dogs and Dad with the lawn mower and head toward the pasture again, hoping that Winnie's right and I can help these horses simply by observing them.

For almost an hour, I observe and take notes. At first, I feel pretty silly.

The gray mare takes two steps. The buckskin's ears go back. The sorrel lifts her head.

But after a while, I see more and start to pick up on interactions. All the buckskin has to do is turn her head, and the others stop grazing. There's a pecking order going on too. I think the Pinto is at the bottom rung.

She takes the bits of pasture the others leave behind.

But what if I'm wrong? I'm afraid Hank and Dakota are going to come home any minute and ask me what I'm doing. I don't know enough about what I've observed to tell them. I need to run everything past Winnie.

It's Tuesday, and I'm pretty sure Winnie mans the Pet Helpline after school. So, armed with pages of notes, I retreat to the house and log on.

KoolKat: Winnie, I don't know if I noticed what I should have, but here goes. The gray mare and the Paint greeted each other by rubbing noses. Maybe they didn't rub, but they did something with their noses. What's that about?

WinnieTheHorseGentler: Great observation, Kat! They probably blew into each other's nostrils. It's a friendly greeting. You should try it sometime. Not with people, but with that pony, Chestnut. If he blows back, you've got yourself a friend.

KoolKat: Wow! I'll try it. Maybe I should try it on the gray mare. I thought she was warming up to me. She seemed to be waiting for me, sticking her head over the fence. But when I walked up to her and reached for her, she backed off fast like she was afraid I'd hit her. I felt horrible.

WinnieTheHorseGentler: She may have been hit at some time. If that's the case, it will take time for her to warm up to you. But it might help to think like she does. Horses have the biggest eyes of any land mammal. They can see all around themselves except right in front and right in back. So when you stand in front of her, she can't see you, and she gets nervous. Try standing to the side of her.

KoolKat: Okay. Sounds good. I observed the bay and the sorrel together. They're so cute. It's a case of I'll-scratch-your-back-and-you-scratch-mine. They used their teeth, but it seemed like they loved it. Not sure what to take away from that, but there you have it.

WinnieTheHorseGentler: Terrific! Horses love to be scratched by people, too. They'd much rather be scratched than patted.

KoolKat: Makes sense. And this is really helping me. But I was kind of hoping I'd come up with something that would help Dakota and Hank get through to these horses. I'm the most worried about the buckskin. She grazes, but she's always watching. When the others get close, her ears go back. If she lifts her head, the other horses keep their distance.

WinnieTheHorseGentler: That's great info. The buckskin is probably your dominant mare. You guys can use that in training!

"Kat? Are you writing Catman?" Hank asks.

He and Dakota are standing behind me at the computer. I can't believe I didn't hear them come in. "You guys scared me half to death." I don't usually use that expression, "half to death," and I can tell by Dakota's face she doesn't like it.

"You're writing Winnie?" Dakota asks.

"About *our* horses?" Hank moves in closer. "Good idea."

"Yeah, really," Dakota agrees.

They're both hunched in front of the screen, one on each side of me. I want to exit from the helpline or cover the screen with my hands or tell them that this is *my* conversation, *my* horse clinic.

"Winnie's right!" Hank says. "That buckskin must be the dominant mare. I was thinking it was the gray."

"So she's the boss?" Dakota asks.

"Yeah," Hank says, still reading. "That's why the others watch her all the time. She's the key, Dakota."

"So we should get her on our side, you mean?" Dakota asks.

They're talking over my head, literally.

"She'll be the one they'll all follow when they're in a pack," Hank explains. "They'll try to please *her.*"

"Ah," Dakota says, "kind of like Guinevere in the pack of girls I tried to eat with today?"

Hank laughs. "Ask Winnie how she thinks we should use the buckskin to get the others on our side. Tell her I've ridden the buckskin, and I think she's pretty teachable."

I start typing, using my two-finger method. I'm slower than usual because my hands are shaky. I'm not nervous. I just haven't eaten much today.

WinnieTheHorseGentler: Kat? Are you still there? Where'd you go?

KoolKat: Sorry about that. Hank and Dakota walked in. They're pretty excited about your advice.

"Go on and ask her about using the dominant mare thing," Dakota says. She pulls over a stool and settles in.

"And tell her what I said about riding the buckskin," Hank adds.

I start to. Then I can't exactly remember the questions. A throbbing starts in my left temple and moves across the top of my head.

"Kat?" Hank sounds impatient.

"Want me to type?" Dakota asks.

I don't. But I don't think I can keep up. I scoot my chair back and stand. "Go for it, Dakota."

"You sure?" She takes the desk chair.

"Thanks, Kat," Hank says. He's staring at the screen. "Huh. Ride the sorrel with the buckskin. We could do that this afternoon."

As I walk away, I hear the computer keys whizzing, Hank's and Dakota's voices, and the buzzing that means I'm in for a king-size headache.

Ten

"Kat, honey? Are you okay in there?" Mom shouts. When I don't answer right away, she knocks on the bathroom door.

It's Friday morning and the first time since Monday that I've gotten dressed for school. I refuse to miss the whole first week of junior high. I wipe my mouth, flush the toilet, and splash cold water on my face. "I'm fine," I call back.

"Hank needs to know if you're riding with him, honey. He and Dakota are leaving in a minute. Wes took the bus. I could drive you later, if you feel up to it." She pauses. "Or maybe you should stay home today and–"

I open the bathroom door and hope I don't look like I feel. "Good to go."

Her eyes narrow. Like it's not hard enough to fool a mom, I have to convince a mom who's also my doctor. "You don't look fine."

"Thanks, Mom. Just the vote of confidence I need to start seventh grade." I move past her and get my book bag. "I'm good. Really."

She doesn't move. "Kat, you don't have to do this."

"Please," I beg. "I don't want to miss any more school."

She sighs, but when I head downstairs, she follows. "Promise to call me if you . . . if you need to come home? I'll keep my pager on. And I'll make sure your dad has his cell on him. I've signed in your meds with the school nurse. So if you need anything for nausea or a headache, just go there."

"I know. Thanks." I really do feel better.

"Hey! Look who's up." Hank takes my pack and slings it over his shoulder. "Riding with me?"

"Yep," I answer.

"Cool hair," Dakota says. "Good choice."

"Thanks." I've gone with the black wig, but it looks brown next to Dakota's hair. I'd love a wig exactly like her hair—curly, thick, black. She looks beautiful in her jeans and a sleeveless T-shirt.

"Let's hit it," I say. "I'd hate to be late for class. Four days late is probably late enough." I kiss Mom good-bye. "Where's Dad?"

At that exact moment, Dad comes running in, panting. "Phone. Mother. Wouldn't let me hang up." He takes a deep breath. "Your grandmother says good luck on your first day at Nice Junior High. She also said to call her if anyone gives you trouble."

I love Gram Coolidge.

We're out the door when Dad hollers, "Wait!"

Dakota rolls her eyes. Hank checks his watch. We all know what's coming.

Dad catches us at the truck. "What do you call a cat who keeps the grass short?"

I've already figured this one out. But I can never leave him hanging. "I don't know, Dad. What *do* you call a cat who keeps the grass short?"

"A lawn *meow*-er! Get it? Lawn meower?"

Dakota groans. She opens the driver's door. "I'll drive."

"Think again," Hank says, dangling the truck key. Dakota's only had her license a week.

I take the front seat without arguing when she climbs in back. Better odds of me not getting carsick if I ride in front. We all know this, but we don't say it. I wish Wes had waited for us. I can't believe he'd rather ride the bus.

Hank starts the truck on the first try. Thinking of that first makes me realize another. "Do you realize this is the first time I've ridden to school with my sister?"

"You and your first times," Dakota mutters.

"Seat belt, Dakota," Hank orders, adjusting his mirrors before backing out.

Dakota buckles up. I'm already buckled. "Listen, Kat," she says, "if you get sick, call me at the high school. I can take the truck and come get you."

"What about me?" Hank asks.

"You can get one of the girls in your fan club to drive you home," Dakota suggests.

Hank laughs. "Fan club? So, are you a member?"

Dakota gives him her "yeah, right" look.

I don't think Hank has an official fan club, but it wouldn't surprise me.

Dakota stares out the window. "Anyway, if I cut classes, it's no big loss." Something in her voice tells me she's not joking anymore.

I glance at Hank. He flashes me a secret-code look. Translated, it means Dakota's not exactly the dominant mare at Nice High.

Dakota's life in Chicago gave her defenses that don't work in our little town. She can come off pretty tough. She and I have gotten along since the day she came to live at Starlight Animal Rescue. But I've seen her A+ sarcasm in action against Wes and Hank. If she felt cornered or put down by people in her classes, I don't think she'd take it in stride. She'd make them wish they'd never opened their mouths.

"Things will get better, Dakota," I say. She's still staring out the window. We've left the rural outskirts of town and turned onto the main drag of Nice. We'll be at the junior high in a minute.

"You know what I hate?" She doesn't wait for an answer. "Hand holding."

"You hate hand holding?" Hank repeats. "Okay."

"Don't get me wrong," she says. "I can be as romantic as the next girl. But please. Like the halls aren't crowded enough? Puppy love has to hold hands so nobody can get by?"

Hank laughs. "Didn't realize you were so anti–hand holding."

But I think I get it. When you don't have a best friend or a boyfriend, it can hurt to watch people who do. Maybe Dakota wishes she had someone.

I know better than to say that to her though.

The picture of a father holding his kid's hand flashes to my mind. "Dakota, I'm giving you a verse for today–a verse about hand holding."

"See? I always thought you had a verse for everything. Now I'm sure." She grins at me, waiting.

"It's from Psalm 37. 'Though they stumble, they will never fall, for the Lord holds them by the hand.'"

Dakota stares at me, her eyes narrowed to slits. For a second, I'm afraid I'm about to be on the receiving end of Dakota's sarcasm . . . for the first time. It's one first I'm not looking forward to. Then, like sunlight bursting out of clouds, she smiles. "Kat, you always know exactly the right thing to say. Do you come in a pocket version? I'd like to take you with me."

"You don't think she's pocket-size already?" Hank says, sounding relieved. He pulls up to the junior high loading zone. Groups of girls huddle all across the lawn. A guy and girl walk by holding hands. Three girls hop out of the car in front of us. Everybody looks high school to me. I was the smallest kid in sixth grade, and I haven't grown much. I probably look like I missed the elementary school bus.

We don't say anything as we sit in the loading zone. Nice Junior High and Nice High School are side by side. The cafeterias overlap even, with a shared central kitchen in the middle. Still, I know it's two different worlds. I don't know what Dakota and Hank are thinking as we sit in the truck, but I'm thinking that all I want is to make it through this school day without getting sick.

My mind kicks into pray-without-ceasing mode, and I open the door.

"Show 'em who's the dominant mare in this school, Kat!" Dakota calls as I climb out.

Hank honks the horn and turns in to the parking lot.

My elbow hurts when I wave, but I keep it up until the truck disappears into the mass of cars trying to park in the student lot. I wonder if Wes is here yet.

I hate the minutes in the hall before that first class begins. Having cancer makes you a bad choice for small talk. Like people are afraid they'll ask me how I'm doing and I'll answer, "Oh, I'm dying, thanks. And you?"

When the first bell rings, I take my time getting to room 121, my first-hour social studies class. I know where it is because Mom and Dad and I met with my teachers during the summer to work out a system for me to make up work when I'm absent.

I stand outside the classroom, listening to the buzz of voices. Their words crash against each other like waves. But the waves are all part of the same ocean. And I'm just passing through their ocean.

My stomach flutters, but I think it's nerves. I sure hope so. The last thing I need is to puke all over the classroom on my first day. I hike up my book bag, walk in, and look around for an empty seat.

"Take your places, ladies and gentlemen!" Ms. Buffenmyer shouts. She's younger than Mom, taller, and a lot thinner. Her brown hair is caught up in a banana clip.

I edge to the middle of the room. Desks to the left, desks to the right. Makes me think of the parting of the Red Sea.

Ms. Buffenmyer is messing with her briefcase, so I don't think she's seen me yet. But everybody else has. I know most of them from elementary school. A couple of kids from church smile at me, and I smile back, but their row is full. Across the aisle, a whole row of girls stare at me. When I smile at them, their heads swivel away in unison, like they're on the synchronized stare team.

Maybe I have a big letter *C*, for "cancer," on my forehead today and didn't notice.

I need a seat. My legs twitch. They shake, like they're not going to stand here another minute. If I don't get a chair, I'm going to collapse in the middle of this classroom.

ELEVEN

FIONA MORRIS STANDS AND WAVES at me from the front of the room. "There's a seat up here, Katharine!" she shouts. "Come sit by me."

I'm surprised she knows my name, even though we had gym together last year. I mostly sat out.

"Katharine!" Ms. Buffenmyer sees me now. "Welcome. Glad you could make it. I mean, it's good to see you."

I walk to the front and take a seat next to Fiona. She's wearing a skirt with a green V-necked top. Her shirt matches her eyes. Her auburn hair flows straight to her shoulders and tucks under perfectly, like those expensive wigs in catalogs. I think she's lived in Nice only a couple of years, but she was the most popular girl in elementary school last year.

"Thanks, Fiona," I whisper.

She pats my hand. "I don't mind," she whispers. "Really, I don't."

I'm not sure why, but having her say she doesn't mind makes me feel like maybe she does. Then she flashes me a smile, and I know I'm imagining things. I'd still be standing in the aisle if she hadn't flagged me down.

Cassie's on the other side of Fiona. I can't believe how much she's changed over the summer. She's streaked her hair, and it looks great. Maybe it's her low-slung jeans and low-cut top, but she could pass for 18.

"Hey, Cassie," I whisper. "I love your hair."

"Thanks. You too." She smiles, but her gaze is stuck on my wig and stays there a few seconds too long. Makes me wish I'd picked the blonde wig instead.

Alex leans up from the seat behind me. He's in my youth group at church, when I feel well enough to go. "Hey, Kat. Cool hair. New?"

I whisper back at him, "Kind of. Thanks, Alex." I could hug the guy for liking my hair. My stomach unclenches. I reach into my book bag for a notebook.

Fiona leans over. "Don't pay any attention to Alex. Boys can be so rude."

I ease back into my seat, clutching my notebook like it will keep me from falling off the earth.

"All right," Ms. Buffenmyer says, "let's get down to business, people. Now, I'm going to need something in writing from you by the end of the hour. You've had a week to think about your social studies project."

As if she's just remembered that I haven't been here all week, our teacher turns to me. "Um, Katharine, we're doing projects in teams of two. Each team has to come up with a civic service project. Teams set goals together, draw up a plan, and do some kind of service for the community. The whole project will be worth a fourth of your grade." A shadow passes over her face, and she steps closer to my desk. "Since you're coming in on this late, maybe you and I can come up with an alternate project, something you can do at home if you want to. A report, maybe?"

I know she's trying to be helpful, but the last thing I want is special treatment. "I'd like to do the civic service project." My voice cracks, so I clear my throat. "It sounds great. Fun. I really want to do it."

"Well . . ." Ms. Buffenmyer draws out the word like she's trying to string thoughts together. "That's a problem. We're doing the work in pairs–partners. I . . . I don't think we have anyone for you to work with."

I hate the silence that follows. They knew I was coming. Why didn't they put me on a team?

"JP, you don't have a partner, do you? I mean, since Ian got his schedule changed?" Meagan Reed announces this from the back of the room. Meagan is probably the smartest person in seventh grade.

JP turns and glares at her, like she's ratted him out. He's wearing a Chicago Bears T-shirt and gray sweatpants. His legs are sprawled out, and his big feet rest on the chair in front of him. JP lives football. It's the only thing I've ever heard him talk about, although he wasn't talking to me. I don't think he's said two words to me in the last two years. In sixth grade, if we heard snoring in class, we all looked at JP.

"I'm doing my own project," JP says.

"And what might that be, Mr. Peterson?" Ms. Buffenmyer asks.

"Football," he answers. He slumps down even farther.

A few chuckles ripple across the room.

"I'm not sure you've quite grasped the assignment, Mr. Peterson," Ms. Buffenmyer says.

"Will you just call me JP? I keep thinking my dad's walked in or something."

"Well, JP," Ms. Buffenmyer says, "you need a partner. And a better idea than football."

"Better than football?" JP whines. "Man, junior high is as tough as my brothers said it was."

More laughs follow. I hate this. Everybody sees that JP and I should make a team. They also see that JP doesn't want *me* for a partner.

"I have an idea, Ms. Buffenmyer," Fiona says. We all look to her like she's the teacher now. "Cassie and I were going to be partners. But, well . . ." She puts her hand on my arm. "Maybe Cassie could team up with JP, and Kat and I could work together."

"Hey!" Cassie objects. "You and I already have our project."

Fiona turns to her friend. "You and JP can do that one. Sounds like JP needs a new project anyway. *And* a new partner. Kat and I will come up with something else."

"That's okay," I tell her, even though I'd love to be her partner. "You don't need to switch partners because of me."

"It's not a problem," Fiona says.

"Cassie really doesn't want to," I whisper.

Fiona whispers back, "Don't kid yourself. Cassie's got a monster crush on JP. She's going to thank both of us later."

"Cassie?" Ms. Buffenmyer says. "What do you say?"

"Well, I guess it might work," Cassie says. She turns around and smiles at JP. "You game, JP?"

He shrugs. "I still think football was a cool idea."

Cassie's already out of her seat and moving in on JP. "Make room, guys. I need to sit by my new partner."

"Good. Now get busy, people." Ms. Buffenmyer strolls toward us. "Thanks, Ms. Morris."

"Glad to help," Fiona says.

"For this to work, though," Ms. Buffenmyer says, "you girls will have to come up with your project by the end of class today. We don't have time for an extension."

"No sweat," Fiona says.

I'm sweating already. I don't want to wreck Fiona's grade. "What were you and Cassie doing for a project?" I ask.

"Nothing terrific," Fiona says. "Her dad owns Nice Pizza in town."

"I didn't know that." We've eaten there a couple of times, but we're too far out in the country for delivery.

Fiona studies her fingernails. They're amazing–long and this bronze color that goes great with her hair. "Cassie and I were going to make up a new specialty pizza with tons of cheese, all kinds of cheeses. We thought we'd promote it for a week and see if we could make a profit. Then we'd give the profit to poor kids or something. Or use the profit to feed poor people. Something like that."

"That's pretty cool," I say.

Fiona shrugs. Her hair swishes, like in those silky shampoo commercials.

Two guys from the second row are trying to get Fiona's attention. When she looks at them, they're pointing to themselves, trying to elbow each other out of the way. "Be on *my* team, Fiona!" one of them whispers. But his whisper is so loud that Ms. Buffenmyer walks over to them.

Fiona shakes her head. Again, her hair flows from side to side.

As I watch her, I can't help wondering what it would feel like to be Fiona Morris. And if I *were* Fiona Morris, I wonder how much I'd regret pairing up with me.

TWELVE

"I GUESS WE BETTER get going on this, huh?" I suggest. "I'm afraid I don't have anything we could sell."

"We don't have to sell anything," Fiona says. Her eyes dart around the room while she talks. "It could be a do-gooder project or a service or something." She waves at a guy I don't recognize. He waves back.

Behind us, Alex and Michael are getting pretty loud. Alex scoots up and asks, "Hey, Katharine. You still like being called Kat?"

I nod. I'm too surprised he's talking to me, and not Fiona, to say anything.

"Are you still running that animal rescue out in the country?" he asks.

"Yep." This is crazy. I've never had trouble talking to Alex before. Last year in youth group we were partners for a scavenger hunt. I puked halfway through the hunt. We lost.

"How'd you like another cat?" Alex asks.

"*I* would. I always want another cat. But I promised I wouldn't take on any more until I find homes for the ones we have."

What I don't tell him is that I know Mom made this rule because I've been sick so much I haven't kept up my end of the work, even with the cats, especially the barn cats. Dakota has had to cover for me. That's why I didn't try to fight the ruling. I hate making extra work for anybody.

"Too bad," Alex says.

"Why?"

"We've got the stupidest cat in the whole world. My mom's going to make me get rid of it if it doesn't come around."

"No way," Fiona says. "*I've* got the stupidest cat in the world."

"I'm serious," Alex insists. "This cat, Bozo—he isn't normal, even for a cat. He pukes all over the furniture. Mom's convinced he does it on purpose."

"He wouldn't do it on purpose," I assure him. "What do you feed Bozo?"

"I don't know. Milk. He likes eggs."

"Well, there you go," I say. "Cats like a lot of things that aren't good for them."

"Just like us girls," Fiona chimes in.

"Milk's not good for a cat?" Alex asks.

I shake my head. "Milk can make a lot of cats sick. Try not giving Bozo milk or eggs. I'll bet he stops puking on the furniture."

"That's great, Kat," Alex says. "But Bozo's got worse problems than that. Like, he licks us all the time." He shudders. "Gives me the creeps."

"Eew," Fiona says, shuddering too.

"You should be flattered, Alex," I assure him. "Do you ever watch cats together? Our barn cats won't let anybody near them except for me. But they lick each other all the time. It's part grooming and part bonding. That's why they lick people, too."

"So Alex's cat thinks he needs to be groomed?" Fiona says, giggling.

"More like his cat really likes him."

"Well, our cat hates us," Fiona says.

"Are you talking about the cat you think is dumber than my cat?" Alex asks.

"Oh, she's dumber all right. I guarantee it." Fiona tugs a strand of her hair. "Mom and I picked out this cat for my little sister for her birthday. It was the prettiest cat in the pet store–long white hair and big blue eyes. That's why we got it."

"So what's wrong with her?" Alex asks.

"She won't listen. She's too stupid to get out of the way of the car. Dad almost ran over the thing twice. Oh, and she gets lost. What kind of a cat gets lost when it goes outside? And we have to carry her to her food dish. She never comes when we call her. We phoned the pet store and complained. The guy finally admitted the cat's already been returned twice! They won't take her back again."

"There's got to be a reason your cat acts like that," I suggest.

"Yeah," Fiona says. "There is. She's dumb as dirt. I'll bet even Catman couldn't help this cat."

"You know Catman?" I can't imagine Fiona and Catman together. I'm not sure why that is.

"I've never met him. But I know he's

Hank's cousin, and he's supposed to be great with cats." A big smile passes over her face. "So how *is* Hank, anyway?"

"Fine, I think." I glance at the clock and know we're running out of time. I don't have time to talk about Hank. And I shouldn't be using up time talking about cats either. But I worry when people don't like their cats. I'm already wondering if Mom would change her mind and let me take on these two cats.

"Your sister loves her cat though, doesn't she?" I ask Fiona.

"Are you kidding? She hates it. She and Mom are taking the thing to the animal shelter over the weekend."

"You can't, Fiona!"

"Why not?" Alex asks. "We're thinking of doing the same thing. Maybe they can find a family the cat will like better than us."

I wheel on him. "Alex, don't let them take your cat there," I plead. "The shelter's over-loaded. They'll never find a home for your cat. Seventy percent of the cats that go into shelters don't come out."

"Man, I didn't know that." Alex taps his pencil on his desk like he's thinking it over. "Maybe I can talk Mom out of it. Do you think you could train Bozo not to claw the furniture? That's the other thing that drives Mom over the edge."

"I don't know." Catman says you don't train cats. You train people. But I did get Ketchup to quit scratching the table legs. I just got him hooked on a scratching post. "Maybe."

"Five minutes left, people," Ms. Buffenmyer announces.

"Fiona, what are we going to do?" I can't believe we haven't even come up with a single idea.

"Your guess is as good as mine." She doesn't sound panicked though. "I could sure use an A in this class. My parents are expecting me to be on the honor roll again."

Alex and Michael get busy writing down their ideas for their project. From what I can hear, it's a garage sale.

Ms. Buffenmyer is making her way toward us. I get the feeling she's been watching us the whole time. "You girls certainly did a lot of talking with the boys this hour. I hope it was about your project."

"Of course, Ms. Buffenmyer," Fiona says. "Alex and I were discussing our projects."

Ms. Buffenmyer raises an eyebrow. It's a skill they must train teachers in teacher school. Every teacher I've had could do it. "Katharine, have you come up with a good idea for your project then?"

"Not really," I admit.

Alex interrupts. "Sorry. My bad. I kept bugging Kat for advice."

"Advice?" Ms. Buffenmyer asks.

"About my cat."

"Your cat?" Ms. Buffenmyer sounds unimpressed.

"Yeah," Alex says. He grins at me. "Kat's a terrific cat shrink."

"I'm sure that's really helpful," Ms. Buffenmyer says, "but not in social studies." She turns to Fiona. "So, Fiona, would you like to tell me what you meant when you assured me you and Alex were talking about your social studies project, when you were actually discussing his *cat*?"

I hear Alex gulp.

But Fiona doesn't miss a beat. "Of course, Ms. Buffenmyer. Because Alex's cat is part of our project. Kat and I will be putting on a cat clinic."

Thirteen

"I HAVE NO IDEA how I pulled that off," Fiona brags to the lunch table full of girls.

I'm sitting across from Fiona. I'm not totally sure how I ended up here. I walked into the cafeteria alone. The smell of hot dogs and pizza, mixed with sweat, made me turn to leave. But Fiona was there. And I guess I got swept along with her.

"Seriously," she continues. "Buffenmyer had me, back to the wall, for goofing off with Alex the whole hour. We were talking about his crazy cat and my stupid cat. So when she pressed me for a project, there it was. Cats!

Stroke of genius." Fiona glances at my plate. "Kat, you haven't touched your lunch. Eat up, girl! We need our strength to pull off the best project in junior high, right?"

"Guess I'm not that hungry." I poke my fork at the pork and beans on my plate. The thought of eating this stuff makes my stomach flip.

"You need ketchup?" Fiona tears open a tiny packet from her tray and squirts red on my untouched hot dog. She tears off one end of the dog that's wrapped in a soggy bun and hands it to me. "There. Eat."

I take a bite and try to smile while I chew. I know better. The smells here are enough to make me sick. The hot dog tastes like rubber.

"That's better." She turns back to her friends. They've waited through the entire hot dog scene. "Anyway, nobody else will have a cat clinic, right? I think we might even ace this thing. My parents would love that. Don't you think it sounds sweet?"

The heads at the table nod like those bobblehead dolls. I think they'd agree with anything Fiona said. Not that I'm complaining. Most of the girls in this room, even the eighth graders, would love to sit at Fiona's table.

Chew, chew, chew. My stomach's shouting at me, warning me not to send this stuff down there.

Fiona turns to me. "I hope you've got tomorrow free."

I nod. And swallow. And swallow again. Chewed-up dog lodges in my throat. "I need to go to the bathroom."

Fiona puts her hand on my arm. "You're a big girl now. You can wait until we're done."

I'm done. She could stick that whole dog in my mouth and I wouldn't eat it. But I don't leave. This is the first time–*first*–I've been asked to sit at a table filled with girls from my class.

My forehead breaks into a cold sweat. The room tilts. The taste of hot dog rises from my stomach and pushes through my nostrils. My head's light. The table spins.

"Kat?"

I look up. "Wes?" I can't believe he's talking to me. Not that Wes doesn't love me, but high schoolers don't want to be caught dead with the junior high kids. Especially not seventh graders who are about to lose their lunch. I'm not even sure it's okay for him to cross over into our side of the cafeteria. But, man, I'm glad he did.

"You've got a call," he says.

"A call?" My heart speeds up. "Why didn't they call my cell?"

"Don't make 'em wait," he warns.

I stand. "Is something wrong?"

"Nothing's wrong. Everybody's fine. Are you going to take the call or not?"

"I'm coming." I scurry from the table and hurry to catch Wes, who's halfway out of the cafeteria already. When I'm in range, I call out, "Wes, who is it?"

"There's no call," he says. "And the closest bathroom is right down there." He points down the hall.

"Thanks, Wes." I dash to the girls' bathroom and make it in the nick of time. I'm loud, retching and retching, the echo four times as loud as at home in my own bathroom, thanks to these gray cement walls.

"Let's get out of here." Footsteps of two or three girls shuffle out. They can't get away fast enough. I can't blame them.

I'm sick again. I can't believe there's anything left inside me. After another minute, I leave the stall and splash water on my face. I lean on the sink, careful not to look in the mirror.

When I finally come out, Wes is at the drinking fountain.

"You're still here?" I can't believe I'm this glad to see him.

Wes wipes his mouth with the back of his hand. "Good thing you came out when you did. If I drank any more water from this fountain, I'd have to run in there and hurl myself."

I laugh a little. "How did you know, Wes?"

"Good guess. That's all."

"It could have gotten pretty ugly in the cafeteria if you hadn't come to my rescue like that," I admit.

He shrugs. "Don't mention it. *Please* don't mention it. You want me to call Popeye to come get you? Or Hank?"

I shake my head. "No. Please don't tell them. It wouldn't help anything."

"Maybe. But you're looking whiter than usual, Kat," he says.

"All I want is to get through the whole day. I can do it. I know I can."

"What do you have next hour?"

"English. Wes, what if I hurl in English class?" I picture it, and the thought almost makes me want to run back to the bathroom.

"Then you give them an English lesson," Wes says.

"An English lesson?"

"Sure. Vocabulary. Vomit vocab. I guarantee you know more words for *vomit* than anybody in that class, including your teacher."

I laugh, but my laugh cuts off when the bell rings.

Wes heads back toward the high school. The halls fill with students pouring in from every classroom door.

"Thanks!" I yell. I can't see him any longer. He's not tall in this crowd.

Then I see a dark-skinned arm rise above the masses, and Wes gives me the thumbs-up sign. Wes may not have the Coolidge name, but he's a Coolidge through and through.

I let myself be swept through the hall to the stairs. Then I make my way to my English classroom.

"Do you have English now?"

I turn to see Alex. He's a lot taller than I thought he was when he was sitting in social studies. Man, that kid has grown. "Yeah. English. Do you?"

He nods. "I've heard Rice is cool."

"Rice? Our English teacher?"

"No. Rice, our lunch." He grins, and I'm pretty sure he's not laughing at me. In fact, I like that he's treating me like a regular person. "So, you going in or watching from out here?"

"I'm going in. And taking *your* seat." It's not that clever, but he laughs anyway.

"Yo! Alexandro! This way!" Michael waves Alex toward an empty seat near the back of the room.

Alex shrugs and takes off to sit with his buddies.

I glance around the room. The good seats, close to the door, are taken. I have to go to the far side of the room and crawl over three kids.

Rice calls roll and dives straight into the romantic poets.

I'm taking notes as fast as I can when the room dips. I look up, half expecting everybody else to be holding on to desks or at least trying to figure out what's happening to us. But they're all writing in notebooks as if nothing's happened.

The wave comes again, bringing full-blown nausea with it. I shove my fist into my mouth and bite.

I have to get out of here.

Rice is writing on the board. "Pay attention to new words in the sonnets. We'll be learning specialized vocabulary. Vocabulary tests will make up 10 percent of your grade."

I need fresh air. Or a toilet.

I get to my feet and start shoving my way out of the row. Then I remember my book bag. I go back for it and climb over desks and people again to get out to the aisle. My head is so light I can't see well. I'm wobbling.

I am not going to make it.

Bile rises to my throat. I burp it back.

"What's the matter with her?" someone asks.

I go down to my knees before I fall. And still my stomach lurches. Frantically I reach into my book bag. My can. I can't find my emergency can. It's got to be here.

I dump my bag out in the middle of the aisle. Chairs near me squeak as people scoot back. Away from me. The can's right there in front of me. The empty coffee can I take with me everywhere. For emergencies. Like this.

No time to be embarrassed. I pull off the lid and stick my mouth over the can. Then I hurl. The sound echoes in the metal can.

"Gross!"

"Eew!"

Groans and disgusted noises surround me.

And still I hurl. And hurl. Everything disappears except the spasms in my stomach. And in my throat. My shoulders heave. My hands shake. I couldn't stand up if I wanted to. And it keeps going until I empty my stomach, my guts, and my heart.

FOURTEEN

WHEN I'M SURE I'M DONE, when there's nothing left inside of me, I still keep my head down, hanging over my coffee can. It helps the dizziness stay away.

Besides, I can't bear to look up. The classroom is silent. I know they're staring.

"Are you okay?" Alex kneels beside me, but somehow he's still towering over me.

"Oh, man," I mutter. I feel in my bag for a tissue and wipe my mouth. *I'm disgusting.*

"Is she okay, Alex?" Rice asks, still at the board. "Katharine, can we call someone?"

"Tell him I'm okay," I whisper, still not looking up.

"She's all right," Alex relays.

"Thanks," I whisper. "I don't want to leave class." I put the lid on the coffee can. For all that noise and effort, there's not much in it.

Alex takes the can from me. Then he gets to his feet and helps me up. I see that he's already repacked my book bag. "She was just kidding. She didn't really hurl. She's trying out for the theater."

There's a little laughter from somewhere.

"Oh, she hurled, all right," Cassie says. Her chair is the closest to me. She scoots it even farther away than she already had. "Trust me. She hurled."

Father, You promised that when I'm weak, You're strong. Well, I'm weak now.

I stand up straight and look at Cassie. "*Hurl?* That's the best you can come up with?"

"What are you talking about?" Cassie frowns at me, then makes a face to the guy next to her, like I'm a lunatic.

Maybe I am. But Wes's idea is making its way into my brain, and I've got nothing to lose.

"I'm talking about *hurling*, since that seems to be the only word you have for it."

"What? You want another word for . . . for what you did? Fine. *Puke*. Like that?" Cassie looks to the guy next to her for support. He shrugs.

"That's all you got?" I ask, like I'm disappointed.

She doesn't answer.

I turn to the rest of the class. "Anybody? What's another word for *hurl* and *puke*?"

Nobody says anything.

For a second, I think about running out of the room and never coming back. *When I'm weak, You're strong.*

"Um . . . *vomit*?" Alex offers.

I smile at him and hope he knows how grateful I am for that answer. "We're getting there."

I walk toward the front of the classroom. My legs tremble, but I don't think it shows. "Mr. Rice, do you suppose I could take a few minutes and share some specialized vocabulary with the class?"

He grins. It's a great grin, like his whole body relaxes into it. "It would be the greatest of pleasures." He hands me a marker for the board. "The floor is yours." He takes a seat on the edge of his desk and waves me to the board.

All or nothing, I think. In big letters, I print: *VOMIT VOCABULARY.*

Laughter ripples across the room.

"Yeah, man!" someone says.

Under my heading, I write *vomit, hurl,* and *puke.*

"Hey, I'm starting to like seventh grade!" somebody shouts.

A girl's voice asks, "Mr. Rice, will this be on the test?"

He quiets the class, and I turn around. "What else? Who knows another way to say *vomit?*"

"Does *throwing up* count?" Margaret asks. I almost didn't recognize her because she cut her hair really short over the summer.

"You bet, Margaret."

She looks surprised that I know her name. We were in fourth grade together.

"Don't want to neglect the obvious," I say while I write *throw up* on the board. "Come on. Don't tell me this is it for you guys?"

"*Blowing chunks!*" somebody shouts from the back. Everybody groans.

"I know. *Barf*!" hollers a girl named Sarah. "That's what my dad calls it."

I write the words on the board, and they keep 'em coming.

"*Lose your lunch?*"

"*Retch.*"

I'm caught up writing, so I wait. "Are you done?" I ask.

"Oooh! Oooh! *Upchuck!*" Danita shouts. She laughs, then adds. "Sounds like rap, don't you think? *Oooh! Oooh! Upchuck!*" The way she says it, it does sound like rap.

This time when I ask for more, I'm met with silence. I wait a minute longer. Then it's my turn. "Not bad. But as you might imagine after today's performance, my family and I know many ways to vomit."

This is met with nervous laughter from a few kids.

"So, first, let me take this opportunity to apologize to the class for not quite making it to drive the porcelain bus."

"The what?" Rice asks.

But a few of the kids are cracking up.

"Porcelain bus, get it?" Michael shouts. "Like, as in the toilet? *Driving* the porcelain bus?"

"Gross!" Cassie says. But it's a different "gross" than the one she said a few minutes ago.

I press on, writing as I go. "Then we've got *hugging the porcelain nurse, bowing at the porcelain throne, talking to Ralph and Bertha on the porcelain phone.* And so on. Eventually you can even make up your own vocabulary."

"Which," Rice chimes in, "is how our language expands. Proceed."

"I believe we forgot *spew*, a concise vocabulary word, for you guys still taking notes."

There's real laughter for that one.

"*Doing the bulimic boogaloo*, which sounds funny but isn't. So don't do it."

The bell rings. A couple of people say, "Aw," like they're disappointed.

I turn to face them. "I'll leave you with a few words to help when you travel. In England, particularly in Birmingham, you will be *currying cufflinks* or maybe *giving a technicolour yawn*. And finally I'll close with a word you can use on your next trip to Scotland, especially if you get seasick. If you're hanging over the side of your boat, grossing out the other passengers, you're probably *honking*."

When school's over, kids are still coming up to congratulate me on my terrific vomit vocab. I wait in the loading zone for Hank, and I replay the instant Alex came to the rescue after the coffee can disaster and the moment I asked God to be strong because I was so weak.

It's hot in the sun, but I smell rain waiting behind gray, bottom-heavy clouds. What a day. I'll have volumes of firsts to write Catman about. First time teaching. Maybe the first time anybody ever has taught vomit vocab.

I watch cars back out of spots in the parking lot and pace the loading zone. I don't see how Hank will ever get through this parking lot mess to pick me up.

"I caught you." Fiona walks up. I think her ride must be here waiting on her because a black car honks, and she holds up a wait-one-minute finger.

"Hey, Fiona." I wonder if she's heard about

English class. I wish she'd been there to see it—not the hurling incident but the vocab lesson.

"Waiting on your ride?" she asks.

"Yeah. I think it will be a while. Parking lot's crazy."

"I wanted to touch base on our project," she says. The black car honks again. So does the car behind it. Fiona shouts, "Be right there!" Then she says to me, "Just so you know, I don't like cats. You're going to have to do the training thing without me."

"People can't actually *train* cats," I explain.

"Whatever." Her gaze darts around the parking lot. "I'll write things up and give the final class presentation and everything. But you've got to do all the cat stuff."

This is sounding better and better to me. "Great. So you really think it's going to work?"

"Better than that," she says. "That pizza sale idea of Cassie's was like half the projects in our class. Make money and give it somewhere. Big deal. But this project? I think it could be the best one if we do it right. Listen, Kat, are you busy tomorrow? 'Cause we ought to get going on this. I could come out to the Rescue."

"*Our* Rescue? Starlight Animal Rescue?"

She laughs. "Makes sense, doesn't it. We're going to *rescue* all the cats, right?"

"Sure." I know I should check with Mom and Dad first. At least, I think I should. I've never had a friend come over before.

Fiona stands on tiptoes and gazes across the parking lot. It's thinning out some. The black car honks. Other cars pull around it and pick up their passengers. Fiona ignores all of them. "So, will Hank be there tomorrow?"

"Yeah. Probably. He rescued eight horses from a trail ride place that got shut down because they abused the animals. I'm sure he'll be working with them all day tomorrow."

"Poor Hank," Fiona says.

"He'll be okay. He's really good with horses."

"He must be a great guy. You're so lucky, Kat."

"I know."

"And his parents must be really nice people too. I mean, how many people take on problem kids and fosters like that? Extra work when you've already got so much to do? You'd think they'd at least get kids who could help out with the Rescue."

I want to tell her that we help, that we all help. Only *not* helping is what's been nagging at me ever since we got the final court adoption date. Fiona isn't saying anything I haven't been saying to myself.

"And Hank's willing to drop you off and pick you up every day. That's pretty cool of him. Not everybody would do that."

The black car's horn honks again, loud and long. This time, Fiona strolls over to it and gets in.

By the time Hank drives up, all I want to do is get home as fast as possible. Hank and Dakota fire questions at me about my first day in junior high, but I'm too tired to go into details. Besides, there doesn't seem to be much to tell. My big "success" in English class feels about as dumb as my big "success" giving the pony his medicine. Neither one amounted to anything worth mentioning.

FIFTEEN

SATURDAY MORNING I sleep in. I don't get out of bed until I hear the dogs going crazy downstairs. The night before, Dad kept talking about the big court date, and Mom spent the evening on the phone with Gram, planning the "Kat Coolidge birthday party."

The whole time, I watched Lion hop on three legs around the kitchen. The dog does fine. Wes rescued the three-legged Pomeranian from Nice Animal Shelter, but he couldn't find a home for him. Now he's saving Lion for his mom, when she gets out of rehab and has a place of her own.

But what I thought as I watched the little dog was how he'd been tossed from home to home, returned because he was too much trouble. And I know that's what would have happened to me if the Coolidges weren't the kind of people they are. *I'd* be the one returned to sender.

The dogs are still barking downstairs. I walk to the banister and peer down. *Fiona!* She and Hank are standing on the front porch.

I dash back to my room and pull on clothes and my wig, brush my teeth, and get downstairs as fast as I can.

"Kat!" Mom calls from the kitchen. "I was just coming to get you. Your friend's out on the front porch with Hank."

I can see them talking, so I slip around to the kitchen. "Sorry I didn't ask if Fiona could come over, Mom. I kind of forgot. I was so tired after school."

"Nonsense. I'm thrilled you have a friend to invite over." Mom smooths my hair. It's the black wig again.

When I walk out to the porch, Fiona's laughing at something Hank said. "Hank, I had no idea you were so funny."

Then I see she's holding a beautiful white cat. "Fiona, hi. Is this your cat?"

"My sister's cat," Fiona answers.

"Where's Wes?" Hank asks. "He should take these dogs on another walk. Maybe they'd stop barking at this poor cat."

"Princess doesn't care," Fiona says, holding out the cat for me to take.

"Anyway," Hank says, one hand on the screen door, "nice to see you again, Fiona. I've got to get back to the barn."

Fiona watches Hank leave, then brushes off her blue silk shirt. "That cat sheds."

"She's beautiful." I stroke her where Kitten loves to be scratched. The cat doesn't make a sound. "How do you get her to purr?"

"Are you kidding?" Fiona says. "That cat hasn't purred since we got it. She doesn't do anything. I told you."

"Doesn't she meow when she's hungry?" I ask, thinking that this cat's eyes are the bluest I've ever seen.

"Nope. My sister has to pick her up and carry her to the food dish. That's how stupid this cat is. You'll see. All she does is sleep." Fiona walks past me into the living room. "Shouldn't we get to work?" Her head rotates as she takes in what she can see of our house. "You guys sure like animals," she observes.

I try to see the room through Fiona's eyes. Cat throws on the big chair. Dog throws on the couch. Horse wallpaper, cat curtains. "You can come in and sit down."

"Would you girls like something to eat? Or a milk shake?" Mom asks.

"No thanks, Mrs. Coolidge," Fiona answers.

"I better go get dressed," Mom says, not correcting Fiona for calling her "Mrs." instead of "Dr." Mom's probably been up for hours, but she's still in her fuzzy blue robe and red slippers. "I'm driving out to check on Mrs. Wilson. See how she's faring after her surgery. You girls have fun."

We sit at the table and Fiona pulls out a notebook. Princess settles on my lap. "I've already drawn up a plan," Fiona begins, opening her notebook. "Basically, Princess here will be your main client. It would be great if you could train her to do something. Anything. You know, like come when we call her, even. Or a trick?"

I still don't like the idea of "training" cats, but I don't want to be negative. Fiona's already put in a lot of work on this project, and I'm lucky to have her as a partner. It's my fault we're getting such a late start on it.

"I don't know how much I can do in one day," I explain.

"You can keep Princess all week. That's all the time we have, remember? So during the week you can have cat shrink appointments. Then we'll have, like, this fantastic grand finale at my house. People will bring their cured cats. And you can tell them more about cats or whatever. And show them what Princess can do and everything. My mother's ordered cat-shaped cakes, and we'll get cat plates and napkins. I'm inviting Buffenmyer for that part so we get credit."

"When?" I have a million questions, but this is the first one that pops out.

"Saturday."

"I'm not sure how much I can do in a week," I admit.

"I thought you'd be excited about this, Kat. I've put in a lot of work on it already." Fiona sounds crushed.

"It's a great plan, Fiona. Thanks for working on it without me. It's just . . . well, whose cats am I supposed to work with?" I stroke Princess, who's been sleeping so soundly on my lap that I check her pulse and make sure she's still breathing.

Fiona doesn't answer. She's staring out the window. I stare too. Hank gets something–a halter, I think–out of the truck and walks back to the barn.

"Where do we find problem cats?" I ask again, trying not to sound desperate.

"The cats? I don't know. The humane society? That shelter where Alex got his? They're loaded with cats. You said so yourself. We could take them back when we're finished with them."

"We can't do that!"

"Fine," she says. "Then you come up with the cats. I'm doing everything else."

I'd love to use cats from the shelter. But no way I'm working with cats and sending them back. And I could never find homes for them that fast. "Okay. We've got Princess."

"Big deal," Fiona says, still staring out the window. "One cat won't get us an A."

She's right. "Alex is having trouble with his cat. Maybe he could bring his." I'm thinking as I talk. "You know, I'll bet a lot of kids in our class have cats. I think Meagan does. The Brewsters have two cats. Don't the Thompsons have a tabby who just had kittens?"

"How should I know?" Fiona says.

"I'm just saying, I'll bet there are plenty of cat owners in seventh grade who wish their cats were better behaved. Maybe we could ask them to bring their cats."

"Works for me," Fiona says, finally facing me again. "You could set up cat appointments after school every day next week. I can work on the big finale for Saturday."

I feel bad that the excitement is gone from her voice. I know it's my fault. "Sure. Good idea."

"On second thought," she says, "I should be the one to set up the appointments. I know more people in our class than you do. They won't tell *me* no. I know. I'll let them bring the cats to *my* house. That'll get them to come for sure. You could come home with me after school and do the cat stuff there. Everybody knows where I live. We can't expect them to drive way out here anyway."

"Would your mother mind having people and cats in her house?" I ask.

"We have tons of room. You could use one of the screened-in porches. But seriously, Kat, you can't miss school. And you'll need to stay in town every day after school too. All week. Monday through Friday. Can you do that?" She stares at me like she's trying to see for herself if I could last all week.

"Sure. Not a problem. I can stay in town after school." I'm trying to sound confident, but problems are crushing in at tiger-force. I have to stay well. And if I pull that off, I still need to find a way home. I can't ask Hank to wait around for me. Not when he's got the horses to see to.

"I can bring you home with me when you're done, Kat," Mom says from the kitchen, like she's been reading my mind. Or eavesdropping. She's dressed in her khaki pants and a white shirt.

Fiona's expression says Mom's been eavesdropping, and Fiona doesn't like it.

"Thanks, Mom," I call.

"Well, I'm off," Mom says. "Your dad's outside playing with that lawn mower. Fair warning. He's got a fistful of new jokes about cats." She searches for her purse. Then her keys. Then she kisses me good-bye and leaves.

Fiona waits until Mom and Dad say their good-byes and Mom drives off. Then she asks, "Is your foster mother really a doctor?"

I nod. I'm not sure I've ever thought of Mom as my foster mother. But that's the reality.

Thinking about this brings back my determination to do something that will make me feel like I'm a good fit in the Coolidge family. Maybe this whole cat clinic is what I've been waiting for. Maybe this is the way to finally be helpful instead of being the one who always needs help.

Kitten scratches at my pant leg, then climbs up the back of the chair until she's on my shoulders. From there, she stares at Princess and hisses at the intruder.

"Be nice, Kitten," I say, trying to pet them both. Kitten keeps hissing. But Princess barely looks at my cat.

"I've written everything down in here,

Kat," Fiona says, standing. "Just read through it. You really don't need me anymore. Why don't I leave you with Princess? You can get started working on her." She moves toward the door. "Dad won't be back for me for another hour. Maybe Hank can show me how he trains horses."

Fiona leaves, and I don't see her until her dad's car drives up and honks. I recognize the black car from the loading zone yesterday.

After a couple more honks, Fiona strolls out of the barn, turning backward twice to wave at Hank.

"Bye, Fiona!" I shout out the window.

But I guess she doesn't hear me because she doesn't tell Princess or me good-bye.

Sixteen

I SPEND THE REST of the weekend getting to know Princess. She's a sweet cat and loves to sit on my lap. The minute I set her down, she goes to sleep at my feet. In my room she curls up on my cat rug and sleeps all night.

During the day, I watch her inside and outside. She seems fearless. Or unimpressed. Lion yaps at her, and she doesn't even blink. No matter what Mustard and Ketchup do, Princess has no interest. She doesn't even wake up when Rex and Wes storm in for lunch.

Fiona's right about one thing. This cat is very, very strange.

Sunday afternoon it rains, so Dad declares family movie time, and everyone settles in by the TV. Dakota and I are on the couch with Mom. I've got Kitten in my lap, and Princess has curled up in Dakota's, surprising both of us.

Dad stands in front of the TV, his chosen DVD behind his back. "Ready? Ta-da!" He whips out his favorite movie, *Old Yeller*.

"Not again, Dad," Hank pleads.

"Didn't we just watch this the last time it rained?" Dakota asks.

"No," Mom corrects, "we watched it the last time it snowed. But Wes didn't watch it with us then."

Wes gets off the floor and checks out the DVD cover. "Man, this is an oldie. Did you guys see the date on this?"

"It's a classic, Wes," Dad says.

"Yeah? Well, not where I come from. I've never heard of it."

Dad's eyes get big. "Are you telling me you've never seen *Old Yeller*? Never ever?"

"So?" Wes challenges.

Rex lets out a little whine to warn Wes he's getting close to anger.

"So, my fortunate, doubly blessed Wes,"

Dad exclaims, "you are in for the treat of your life!"

Wes shakes his head. "Thanks. I think I'll pass. Again."

"There are dogs in it, Wes," I say. I want us all to do this together. Rain pounds the roof. Wind rattles the windows. It's a perfect day for a family movie.

"I don't know, Kat," Dakota says. "Wes would probably cry."

"Yeah, right," Wes says.

"Bet you tonight's chores you can't make it through the whole movie without tears," Hank says.

"Are you kidding? You're on." Wes and Rex scoot back on the floor so Wes can lean against the couch. Hank takes the other side, and Dad sits at Mom's feet, even though there's a recliner empty at the other end of the couch.

When the movie's over, Hank's won his bet easily, although Wes claimed he had something in his eye that made him tear up like that. He can't get outside fast enough. "I'll grain your horses anyway," he calls back.

Hank jogs out after him. "I'll do the pony,

Wes. Besides, I want to see Starlight, and she'll want to see me."

Hank always says that, even though his horse can't see.

His horse can't see. Can't see . . .

Something's stirring in my brain. What if . . . ?

"Kat?" Dakota whispers. "I need to get up, but I don't want to disturb this cat. I can't believe she sat on my lap the whole movie."

"Wait," I whisper back. I slide to the floor in front of Dakota and Princess. I'm kneeling, facing them, inches from Princess's face. "Now jiggle."

"Excuse me?"

"Jiggle Princess awake."

Dakota moves her knees up and down, jiggles her legs, and jostles Princess until she opens her eyes. The cat shows no surprise seeing me in front of her. "Now what?" Dakota asks.

I raise my hands, making cat claws in front of Princess.

"What are you trying to do? Scare the poor thing?" Dakota asks.

"Something like that," I answer. I back up a foot. "Go ahead and set her down."

Dakota sets Princess on the carpet. The cat stretches, then starts to walk away. I move in directly behind her and clap my hands. "Scat!" I yell.

"Kat!" Dakota shouts.

Again I clap and yell inches from Princess's tail. "Shoo! Scat!"

The cat stops and stretches again.

"Want to tell me what's wrong with you?" Dakota asks.

I sigh. Tears push at the backs of my eyes. I turn to Dakota. "Nothing's wrong with *me*." I lie down beside Princess and stroke her long fur. She can't purr because she's never learned how. She's never *heard* purring. She's never even *seen* another cat. "Dakota, this cat is blind and deaf."

That night I e-mail Catman about Princess. I'm pretty sure I'm right about this cat, but I want to hear it from the Catman himself. Even though he can't study Princess in person, I know he'll be able to help me. I tell him everything I know about the cat, including what Fiona said about other families returning the cat to the pet store because they thought she was dumb.

I keep checking my e-mail until I get an answer an hour later:

Hey, Kat!

Sorry I wasn't here. I needed some follow-up footage of a Persian cat in Polk, Ohio. Far out, man!

Anyway. To cat business. Way to nail this one, Kat! You're right on, man. Your Princess cat's seeing no evil and hearing no evil.

You said Princess has long white hair, right? No dark fur anywhere? There's your proof. Like half of all totally white cats are totally deaf. It's a genetics thing, man. Like calico cats being chicks. (Okay, officially one in 3,000 calicos could be a guy.) Bet Princess has blue eyes too. Go figure, the gold or green-eyed cats have a better shot at hearing.

Come back at me if you're online.

The Catman

As soon as I see Catman's message, I start typing:

Thanks! Sad to know, but good to understand this cat. Poor thing's been bounced around like a tennis ball. At least now we know why she's so weird.

I've got another problem, Catman. For the cat clinic I told you about yesterday (and thanks for the vote of confidence), I'm supposed to teach this blind and deaf cat something, like a trick. Any ideas what I could teach a blind and deaf cat to do . . . in just a week?

Freaking out,

Kat

Catman's answer comes back in seconds:

Teach Princess how to use the john.

SEVENTEEN

MONDAY MORNING Fiona grabs me in the hall and drags me into Ms. Buffenmyer's classroom before school starts. "Good. You're early for once. We have six clients signed up already, and I haven't even made the problem-cat announcement yet."

"Wow! That's great, Fiona."

"I guess." She doesn't sound enthused. "It's just that I'm hearing about these other do-gooder projects, like starting a soup kitchen–"

"Somebody's starting a soup kitchen? That's amazing."

"Right. And we're training cats. I'm

starting to think we blew it, going with this cat thing."

I'm catching her disappointment like it's the flu. "So what do we do?"

"It's too late to change now."

Fiona and I plop into the same seats we had Friday. I was sick around five this morning, but I'm pretty good now. And I'm *not* going to miss school, not this week anyway.

She sighs. "We're stuck with cats. Some social project. We'll probably get a lousy grade. We're not helping *people*. Just their stupid cats. I should have stuck with pizza. At least that would end up getting money for the poor. We won't make a dime on this project."

I can't believe how fast she switched from loving the idea to hating it. She's probably right, though. We're supposed to help people. I lean back in my chair and wonder why I ever thought I could help people or cats.

"Anyway," Fiona continues, "we're stuck. We'll have to make the best of it. Alex is bringing his cat to my house after school. And Cassie wants to bring hers today too."

"I didn't know Cassie had a cat."

Fiona shrugs. "Me either. She probably

bought one so she wouldn't be left out. Before I knew what a waste this cat thing was going to be, I told her about the big finale at my house Saturday." Fiona glances around the room until she sees someone and waves. She gets up. "I'm going to go sit with Cassie and Brett. If we don't bump into each other before school's out, be in the loading zone, okay? My mom will pick us up."

I don't get a chance to talk to Fiona the rest of the day, although several kids tell me they're signed up for "cat therapy." Fiona's lunch table is filled when I walk into the lunchroom. And anyway, the second I step into the cafeteria, I lose my appetite.

✯ ✯ ✯

After school, we meet up in the loading zone. Her mom is first in line, but I wait until Fiona comes out. I've met Mrs. Morris before, but I don't think she recognizes me.

We get in, and her mother introduces herself. "I guess we'll be seeing a lot of you this week."

"It's nice of you to let us do this at your

house, Mrs. Morris," I say, still hunting for my seat belt. "Thanks."

"It's nothing, dear. I'm sure your mother wants you to get an A as much as I want Fiona to. It may seem like college is a long way off to you girls, but it's right around the corner."

"Brett's coming over later," Fiona tells her mother.

"Does he have a cat?" I ask.

Fiona laughs. "Brett? A cat? He's trying to get rid of his little brother. I can't imagine him with a pet. He's coming to hang out with me." She checks her notebook. "Alex will probably get there before we do. He's walking. Then you've got Matt, who's been trying since fifth grade to get me to go out with him. And Cassie."

I thought I might have one or two cats to see. Not three. I've been praying for a second burst of energy—and a third and a fourth—since noon. Plus, I want to get back for another toilet-training session with Princess. I'm not mentioning that to Fiona. It will be a surprise if it works. And I won't have to let her down if it doesn't.

Fiona flips down the car visor and puts on pink lip gloss. "Watch the bumps, will you, Mother?"

"Sorry," Mrs. Morris replies.

Fiona's house is one of the newer homes in Nice–white brick, sprawled over two lots. I've been by it dozens of times. It's right up the street from Nice Elementary. Fancy-shaped evergreens don't quite hide it from the road.

"Your house is so nice," I say. "I mean, beautiful." When you live in Nice, you try not to use the word *nice*, even when it fits.

"Thank you, Katrina." Mrs. Morris says my name wrong. I wait for Fiona to correct her, but she doesn't. "The house is a mess right now. We're rebuilding the pool. Workmen track in day and night. But you and the cats should be safe and private on the east porch. Isn't that what you were thinking, Fiona?"

Fiona is already out of the car and halfway up the long drive. "This way, Kat!" she calls without turning around.

Fiona's sister, Arianna, is watching what looks like a soap opera when we walk in. She doesn't turn around.

"Arianna, you know Katrina, don't you?" Mrs. Morris says.

"It's Katharine," I tell Mrs. Morris. "You can

call me Kat if you want. Hey, Arianna. How's sixth grade? Do you have Mrs. Albertson?"

"Hey," she calls without taking her gaze from the TV, where a man and a woman are arguing.

I wait a few seconds, but she doesn't answer the school questions. And she doesn't ask about her cat, Princess.

"Kat?" Fiona calls.

I follow the sound of Fiona's voice and find her in a sunny porch off a room that looks like a library. "This is perfect." I step down onto tiled floor. The room forms a circle with windows all the way around. Outside, workmen are painting an empty pool. The doorbell rings, and chimes echo through the house—some classical song I should probably know.

"That's Brett," Fiona announces. She starts for the door, then turns back. "I'll send the cat people to you when they come, okay?" She tosses the notebook with the names of the cats and their owners in my direction.

I grab it and nod. I'd give just about anything to have Catman here with me. Again I picture the image in that psalm, the kid holding

Dad's hand. Only I picture me holding God's hand. And I'm holding a cat. It helps.

Seconds later, Alex walks in with a big, fat tabby cat. "Man, you could get lost in this house."

"Hey, Alex. And this must be Bozo."

I sit in the chair closest to the couch, and Alex takes the couch. The tabby hangs over his arm like a towel. "So this is cat therapy," he says, glancing around the porch. "I feel like I should lie down on the couch and tell you all my troubles, doc." He fakes lying back. We both laugh.

"Why on earth did you name this sweet cat Bozo?" I ask, scratching the tabby behind the ears.

"Pretty bad, huh? I mean, how smart is anybody going to be if he starts out life as Bozo, right?"

I shrug because I agree with him.

"My dad's crazy about that old clown Bozo who used to be on TV. I'm just lucky they didn't name *me* after that clown."

Neither of us says anything for a minute.

Then Alex says, "Oh yeah. I almost forgot. Your magic's working already."

"No magic here," I interrupt. "I just watch cats."

"I know. I'm just kidding. But what you said about Bozo puking? We stopped giving him milk and eggs, although I think Dad still sneaks him scraps when we're not looking. Anyway, the cat stopped puking. Or should I say doing the technicolor yawn?"

"That's great, Alex." We smile kind of lamely at each other. "Thanks again for helping me out in English."

"Anytime," he says. "I mean, not that you'll do that again anytime. Not that you couldn't if you wanted to. I mean, needed to."

I think Alex is having as much trouble talking to me as I am to him. I wish Fiona were here to help keep the conversation rolling.

Bozo is still hanging over Alex's arm.

"Um . . . what's the biggest problem you need help with?" I ask. "For Bozo, that is. Is it the licking? Didn't you say your cat licks you guys and it creeps you out?"

Alex grins, showing straight, white teeth that make me want to hide my not-so-straight, not-so-white teeth. "Everybody's okay with the licking thing since I convinced them it was

Bozo's way of kissing. Dad claims Bozo likes him best because he's the most licked."

"That's good, then."

"Yeah. But Bozo's still scratching furniture. He loves Mom's best chair. And her great-grandmother's tea table. We've got to get Bozo to stop scratching."

Scratching furniture was one of the first problems I had to learn to handle when I started rescuing cats. "I think I can help Bozo with that one."

"Cool." He hands over the cat. "Be my guest."

I take Bozo from Alex. "You are one big boy," I mutter.

"Thank you," Alex says. He laughs. "Seriously, Kat, why does Bozo scratch Mom's furniture?"

"Cats have sweat glands between their paw pads." I hold up Bozo's paw and show him. "Scratching lets him leave his scent around. So he's saying, 'This couch? That's mine. This expensive table? Mine. This guy named Alex? Mine.'"

He laughs again. "You're right. He scratches us, too. Mom thinks if we're going to keep Bozo, we should declaw him."

I shake my head. "Terrible idea. Cats need their claws. It's their best defense."

"Yeah, but we don't let him outside. Even Mom knows that wouldn't be fair, sending him into the world without his weapons."

"Even inside, Bozo *thinks* he needs those claws. If he doesn't have that clawing defense, he'll probably start biting."

"Not good," Alex admits.

"Declawing cats is illegal in England because it's so cruel," I explain.

"So how do we teach him not to scratch?" Alex asks.

"We don't. Cats *have* to scratch. It's their nature. What we can do, though, is teach Bozo *what* to scratch."

For the rest of the time, I give Alex ideas on how to get Bozo not to scratch the furniture. "I wish we were at my house so you could see some of the things Dad and I have rigged up for our cats. Dad made a scratching post by covering a box with carpet. Ketchup, one of our rescues, loves that thing. Mustard, on the other hand, prefers this log we set up. It's just a regular log, but that cat spends hours scratching at it."

Alex actually writes down my other tips: Dangle toys from the scratching post. Smear the post in catnip. Put the scratching post near the furniture Bozo likes to scratch but drop treats near the post to make it more tempting.

"You can put balloons on furniture you want Bozo to leave alone. It usually takes only one big pop to make a cat leave something alone forever. But you have to stay close by so you can get rid of the popped balloon before he tries to chew it."

"You guys done?" Fiona asks. She and Brett are standing in the doorway of the porch, Brett's arm around her waist. "Because, as they say in the cat shrink business, 'I'm sorry, but your time is up.'"

"I can't believe how fast that hour went," Alex says.

I stand and walk him to the door. "I hope it helped."

Fiona takes over. "And even if it didn't, please say it did." She hands him a sheet of paper. "Here's an evaluation form. Give it back to me when you're done. It's part of our project. I know this is a stupid project, Alex, but it's all we've got."

"Stupid?" Alex glances at me. "I thought it was—"

"Whatever," Fiona says. "Just fill out that evaluation. And try to say something good about how helpful this was. Blah, blah, blah." She's still giving him instructions as they disappear down the hall.

Within minutes, Fiona brings Matt back. He's carting a tiny black cat that looks like she couldn't give anybody problems. When Fiona leaves with Brett, Matt stares after her so long that I have to call him back to earth. This is definitely going to be tougher than the Alex and Bozo act.

EIGHTEEN

"I DON'T KNOW WHAT Fiona sees in that guy," Matt mutters. His cat springs out of his arms, and I don't think Matt even notices.

"Matt?" I scramble after Squirt. Twice, she squirts through my arms, making me wonder if that's how she got her name. But when I get hold of her and sit back on the couch, she purrs for me.

"Squirt is a sweetheart." The more I stroke her, the louder she purrs. "What could possibly be wrong with this cutie cat?"

Matt launches into a list of wrongs, a dozen grievances he and his whole family have against poor Squirt. "You should see what that cat does while we're gone. Mom gets home from work or I come back from practice and the whole house is a mess."

"Matt," I begin, stroking the smooth, black hair on the cat's skinny body, "what you've got here is a latchkey cat."

"You mean like a latchkey kid? When kids come home after school and lock themselves in because their parents are still at work? Kind of like my brothers and me, I guess." He cocks his head at me. "I've never heard of latchkey cats, though."

"Well, you've got one." Squirt is purring up a storm in my arms and rubbing her cheek against my hand. "This sweet kitty doesn't like being left alone. Cats are curious. If you don't leave fun things for her to get into, she'll make her own fun. And you probably won't like it."

"No kidding," Matt says. "Well, what fun could I leave her? She's got more toys than I had when I was a kid. We always leave those out for her. But she'd rather tear up the newspaper or get into the plants."

"Okay. Try this. Tomorrow, put half of the cat's toys away where she can't find them.

Leave a couple out. Then hide the rest in places she can find easily. You could put one in a paper bag. My cat could play with a paper bag all day. The next day, switch toys, bringing out the ones she hasn't seen for a while."

"Cool." Matt's nodding his head. "Kind of a lot of trouble, though."

"Cats take work. And be sure your cat can see out the window without climbing your plants. Pull a table over, or get a card table and put a pillow on it. Anything that will let Squirt watch the birds and see the outside world. She'll do that for hours, which means she won't be getting into trouble, right?"

"Yeah. But I don't know if Mom will want me moving things around. Sounds like a hassle."

I feel like giving Matt and his whole family a lecture on taking time to care for pets. "Here's one I don't think you'll feel is too much trouble. Leave your smelliest T-shirt out for Squirt when you go to school in the morning."

"I can do that," Matt promises.

When Matt leaves, I feel pretty useless, even to the cats. I'm sure Matt came for Fiona, not for his cat. Maybe Alex did too.

I'm glad to have a few minutes to myself before the last cat shows up. My throat feels sore, but I think it's because I'm so tired. When I sit down, my knee hurts, and my legs feel like they're filled with molasses.

"Here she is," Fiona says, leading Cassie into the porch. "The doctor is in."

"Aren't you staying?" Cassie demands.

"Brett and I are busy," Fiona answers. She hands Cassie an evaluation form. "Don't forget to give us a good report. I need that back by Friday."

The whole time Cassie and her cat, August, are with me, I pray that I won't have to run outside and hurl. It's hard to focus on August.

"My mother says if August keeps jumping up on her kitchen counters, she's getting rid of him. She'll do it, too," Cassie promises.

I'm grateful this is a pretty easy fix, because I have only half of my brain power for it. The other part of my brain is trying to talk my stomach out of doing what it feels like doing. "Aluminum foil," I tell her.

"Aluminum foil?" Cassie sounds like she suspects I'm crazy again.

"You cover your kitchen counters with aluminum foil for a couple of days. When August jumps up, he won't like the sound or the feel of foil. Cats hate the stuff. You should be okay to take the foil off after a day or two."

"What if my mother doesn't want to have her counters decorated with foil?" Cassie demands.

"Some people use double-sided sticky tape, but I like foil better. Or you can go with smells, if your mom doesn't want to do the foil thing. Cats hate the smell of vinegar, raw onions, lemon peel, menthol, and stinky perfumes. Put lemon peels on the counter, and your cat won't go near them."

Even thinking about lemon peels makes me want to puke. I bite the inside of my cheek because that helps. Who knows why.

Mrs. Morris comes out to the porch. "I believe your mother's here for you. Someone's honking."

Honking? I almost run to the van. We make it out of town before Mom has to pull over and let me do the honking by the side of the road.

Tuesday I stay in bed the whole day. I hate letting Fiona down, but all I can do is sleep the day away. I leave her messages, but she doesn't call back.

Wednesday morning when I come downstairs, Mom and Dad are talking about our big court date. They fill me in on everything, but I only half listen. I can't help the feeling I get whenever they talk about the adoption being final, about me being a Coolidge. There's nothing I want more, but there's nothing I deserve less.

"We can all fit in the van," Mom says. "We should drive in early, maybe stop by Nice Donuts first and—"

"Saturday morning?" I don't know why I haven't thought of this before now. "Saturday morning I've got to be at Fiona's for our project. Our teacher's going to be there and everything."

"What?" Dad sounds horrified. "But the courthouse! Our court date! It's the only time they do adoptions in this county."

"Easy, my love," Mom says. "What time is your project?"

"I'm not sure. Fiona and her mother are planning it."

"Well, I'm sure it will all work out," Mom says. "Not to worry. One of us can drive you to Fiona's and wait for you. You can meet up with us at the courthouse. It will all work out."

"You are such a level head," Dad tells her.

I ride to school with Hank and Dakota. All the way there, I stare out the window. I don't want to stand before a judge and lie about how I deserve to be a real Coolidge. I don't want to make Mom and Dad lie about it either. Maybe this project at Fiona's will be my way out.

☆ ☆ ☆

Fiona doesn't hide her feelings about my missing school yesterday. "Kat, I asked you in the beginning if I could count on you, and you said I could." We're standing in the middle of the hall before first hour. Kids walk around us and stare.

"I know," I say. "And I'm sorry. I'll be here the rest of the week."

"Well, you better. I told yesterday's cat

owners to come back today. I had every-thing scheduled, and you threw it off by not showing."

"I can–"

But Fiona's too mad to hear me out. We don't talk the rest of the day until we're sitting in her mother's car after school.

"Have you set a time for Saturday's finale?" I ask.

Fiona's mom answers, "The invitations say 10:00. Fiona, didn't you give your friend an invitation?"

Fiona sighs for an answer. "She doesn't need an invitation, Mother. She's the one they're coming to hear talk about cats."

✶ ✶ ✶

Cats file in and out of my "cat shrink" office at Fiona's all afternoon and evening. Cat problems range from a runaway cat to a cat who con-stantly gets underfoot. I have to phone Mom and ask her to pick me up later than planned.

My last client is Mikayla Noel, a girl who goes to our church. She brings Socrates, a sleek female Siamese.

"You know I love animals," Mikayla says. "All animals, including the birds Socrates has been killing in our backyard. I can't stand it anymore. Sometimes she leaves them on our step. Otherwise, she's such a great cat. I don't know what to do to get her to stop killing things, though."

"Cats are hunters," I tell her. "You can't change that. But we *can* make Socrates a bad hunter."

Together, Mikayla and I rig a collar with two bells and a mirror. When we're done, we put the collar on Socrates.

"There you go, Socrates," I tell her. "Now those backyard birds are going to get fair warning when you're on the prowl. Hunting is about to get a whole lot tougher." .

* * *

On Thursday Mrs. Morris picks me up, but Fiona stays for cheerleading practice. I see three cats and get home earlier than usual.

Friday I ride home with Fiona, but she disappears as soon as we get to her house. I see four cats, including Berta, a short-haired gray brought in by Stephen Kirk, an eighth grader.

"I hope it's okay to come, even though I'm not in your class," Stephen says. "Alex told me you can cure any cat, and mine needs help."

I can't believe Alex told him about me. "I don't know about curing any cat, but I'll try. What's up with Berta?"

"She's an unwanted alarm clock in our house. Berta jumps on our beds at dawn and won't stop yowling until we're up."

I like the way he's holding his cat. I can see how much he cares about her. "All I can do is give you some ideas to try. Okay?"

He nods. "I'll try anything."

"Play with your cat right before you go to bed. Tire her out. Feed her later too. That way her stomach won't wake her."

"Okay," Stephen says. "Anything else?"

"If that doesn't work and you're desperate, you could have a hair dryer by the bed, or one of those little car vacuums. If your cat comes in too early, you can surprise her with a noisy blast of air. Only do it as a last resort. It shouldn't take more than once or twice.

Bottom line, Stephen: it's cool that your cat wants you up to play with her."

I actually feel pretty good watching Stephen and Berta leave . . . until I meet Fiona on my way out.

"You know he doesn't even count, don't you?" she snaps as soon as she closes the door on him. "He's not in seventh grade. I couldn't give him an evaluation."

"Sorry, Fiona," I say. But I'm not sorry I got to try to help Stephen and Berta.

"Yeah. Well, look at the bright side. After tomorrow, this whole thing will be over, one way or the other."

NINETEEN

AT HOME, my secret project with Princess is coming right along. Dakota catches me in my room before dinner. "Want to explain to me why I'm sharing the john with a cat?"

I stare at her. "No way. You're not telling me Princess used the toilet."

Dakota nods.

"Seriously? You saw her?" I can't believe it worked.

"Twice," Dakota answers. "Craziest thing I ever saw. How did you get her to do that, Kat? I mean, I saw the litter box on the toilet Monday. Then I saw when you took that away and covered the seat in plastic wrap. Gave me flashbacks to pranks in one of the foster homes I ran away from."

"Catman told me how to do it. I only had to put litter on the plastic wrap for one day."

"Yeah. That was pretty gross."

"I know. And thanks for letting me use our bathroom for Princess. Can you believe how fast she learned? Yesterday she went with just the plastic wrap on the toilet. I took that off this morning. And she's got it already? Unbelievable!"

"And all of this so you and I could have a third party share the bathroom with us?" Dakota's grinning, though. "Seriously, Kat, you're amazing. I expect Princess to be demanding her own reading material in there before long."

"Not our problem after tomorrow," I tell her. Something clenches inside every time I give up one of the rescues. I feel the same way about Princess.

"Well, you did good, kid," Dakota says.

"Princess did, anyway. And she learned all of this blind and deaf. She must be a really smart cat, Dakota. Fiona and her sister will have to see that now."

"What did Fiona say when you told her Princess was blind and deaf?" Dakota asks.

I don't answer.

"You haven't told her?"

"I was hoping I'd have some good news to go with the bad," I explain. "And now I do."

Dakota squats down to stroke Princess. "Good news, bad news, huh? That reminds me . . . Chestnut wasn't limping at all today."

"Really? That's great. He's finished the bute, too, right? So that's good news." But I can tell by her face that the bad news isn't far behind.

"Hank thinks we might have a buyer for Chestnut," she says.

Again, there's that pinching inside me. That's the way it is when you rescue. Your goal is to get the animal to a place where you can find a great home for him. And when you do, it hurts like crazy.

☆ ☆ ☆

After dinner I go out and visit Chestnut. He's in the pasture with the other horses.

Hank walks up behind me. "He looks good, doesn't he? He's not limping at all."

Chestnut comes up to the fence, and I reach in and pet him. I pull up grass and feed him. "Dakota says you might have a buyer."

"It's a family with a little girl who's crazy about horses. She's been riding at a stable for two years. It's a good home. And they've got a neighbor who might want the sorrel."

I pull up more grass and stick it through the fence. Chestnut devours it. It's the same grass he's got on his side of the fence, but it always looks greener this way. I'll miss this pony.

"You getting excited about the adoption deal? I hear Gram wanted to invite the entire state to celebrate." Hank puts his arm around my shoulders and squeezes. "You've been my sister since the day you came here. But I'm glad it will finally be official."

It's all I can do not to cry. "I can't go to the courthouse, Hank."

"Right," Hank says. When I don't chuckle with him, he asks, "You're not worried about that school thing, are you? Dad got the court date bumped to 11:00."

"I don't know if I'll be done by then." I don't look at Hank. I think I'll fall apart if I do.

"Well, *be* done! This isn't something you

can miss. What if they can't make it official unless you're there to speak for yourself or to sign the adoption papers or something? Did you think of that?"

"Yes."

Hank turns me to face him. "Kat? What are you saying? What's going on with you?"

I don't know if I can explain it. I don't know if I want to. I shrug and look away.

"Is there some reason you don't want the adoption to be final?" Hank asks. "Are you thinking about your biological parents?"

I frown at him. "Is that what you think?"

"I don't know what to think. You're blindsiding me here. But you better get it out. Are you . . . are you having second thoughts about us?" I can hear the pain in his voice.

"Hank, no. That's not it. Who wouldn't want to be adopted by your family?"

He doesn't move.

"I just . . . I don't want them to do it out of pity."

"Pity? Kat, they love you. We all love you. How can you not know that?"

"I do know that. But they can love me without giving me their name. *Your* name. It's too big of a gift. I don't want them to do it because they think they have to, because they feel sorry for me."

"Sorry for you?" Hank asks.

"Yeah, sorry for me. I'm too sick and too weak to do anything around here. You should know that better than anybody."

"Kat, this isn't you talking."

"If I could *do* something—something to make me feel like I'm not just a burden to everybody . . ."

Hank shakes his head. "Have you talked to Mom and Dad about this?"

"No. And you have to promise me *you* won't. Promise me, Hank."

He's quiet a minute. "Okay. But have you at least talked to God about it?"

That takes the wind out of me. I'm usually the one telling everybody else to talk to God about stuff.

Out in the pasture, something stirs. The gray mare squeals. One of the other horses has his ears back and looks ready to fight.

Hank leaps into action and vaults the fence. "I'm driving you to that courthouse!" he shouts. "I'm not giving up my sister that easy."

TWENTY

WHEN I COME DOWN for breakfast on Saturday, Mom and Dad are waiting, arm in arm, at the foot of the stairs.

"There she is!" Dad exclaims. "Our own Kat Coolidge."

"I wish you could ride with us to the courthouse instead of coming later with Hank," Mom says.

"Mom, I told you–," I begin.

"Not that we don't understand," Dad says.

"Because we're understanding parents," Mom adds, winking at Dad.

I've told them I don't know if I can make it there or not. But they won't hear it.

"George called me," Mom says.

"Mother called you?" Dad sounds hurt that he didn't get a call from Gram.

"We're all set for the Made-Rite as soon as we finish at the courthouse. I'm glad you kept it just family, Kat. I don't want to share you with anybody."

I hug both of them, and they hug me back. Then I push away and get Princess. "Hank, we better go."

In the truck, Hank makes small talk. "You and Dakota will be sad to see that cat go. Did you really teach it to use the toilet?"

I nod. But I know Hank's thinking about the same thing I am. "I can't go to the court-house, Hank."

"Kat–"

"I don't want to talk about it anymore."

He pulls up at Fiona's and shuts off the engine. "I'll wait right here for you."

"Don't. I need you to go to the courthouse for me."

"You can't–"

But I don't let him finish. I know what I'm

doing, what I *have* to do. "I'm going to put on the best cat clinic anybody has ever seen. Tell Mom and Dad I'm sorry. But this is something I have to do." I climb out of the truck. Princess is still asleep in my arms.

"Kat?" Hank calls after me. "I can't just leave you here."

I turn to face him, but I keep walking backward, clinging to Princess. "You have to. If you ever want me to be ready for the adoption, you've got to let me do this." Then I turn around and don't look back.

On the front step, I ring the bell. Music is blaring from inside. Mrs. Morris opens the door, looking older, with lopsided hair and no makeup.

"It's you, Katrina." She lets me in. "You can be glad you couldn't make it to the sleepover."

"Excuse me?"

"I know you had to get your rest. Fiona said you needed to recharge before today. You wouldn't have gotten a bit of sleep here."

Nobody said a word to me about this sleepover. Couldn't Fiona have asked me, at least? A sleepover. I've never even been to one.

"I'm so proud of Fiona," Mrs. Morris says, leading me through the maze of a hall. "You know, for volunteering to be your partner in this project. She's usually very competitive."

I must have asked myself a hundred times why Fiona volunteered to be my partner. I guess I have my answer. I was her own little good-deed project.

We stop at the door to a big room I haven't seen before. Fiona and Brett are laughing together in one corner. Girls are sprawled out on the floor and couches. A couple of Fiona's cheerleading friends are still in their matching pj's.

Mrs. Morris leaves Princess and me in the doorway.

I picture myself clinging to Princess with one hand and reaching up for my Father's hand with the other. Then I walk in.

Fiona hollers at me. "Finally! Kat, come here."

I glance around and see only three cats. Alex has his Bozo. He waves at me. I wave back, then join Fiona. "Where are the rest of the cats?"

"I told people they didn't have to go home

and get their cats. Buffenmyer can't come, so she won't know anyway."

Fiona barely glances at Princess before shouting, "Hey, everybody! Let's get this over with."

A couple of girls groan. The cheerleaders don't budge from their makeshift bed on the floor. Somebody bursts out laughing from the other side of the room, where it looks like they're playing cards.

This whole thing is so lame. *I'm* lame. What did I think I could do here? The only reason I'm here at all is because Fiona had pity on me.

Fiona shoves me to the front of the room. "Go!" she whispers.

I stand in front of the stone fireplace and look out at my classmates. Only I can't remember what I was going to say.

"Kat?" Alex says. He's moving to the front. "You okay?"

"Oh, great," Cassie says. "Is she going to puke again?"

"Gross!" Arianna shouts.

I clear my throat. I'm *not* going to hurl.

"Somebody ask her a question," Fiona suggests.

"I've got one," says Melissa, a friend of Fiona's. "My cat hates me. What have you got for that?"

I stare at her. Her cat doesn't hate her. Should I say that?

"Kat?" Fiona says, like she's had it with her good-deed project.

I turn back to Melissa. "Well, try to think like your cat."

"What?" Melissa snaps. "I can't hear her."

Before Fiona can tell me to speak up, I do. "Do you pick up your cat and hold her on your lap?"

"I do that," Melissa insists. "But she won't sit and watch TV with me. She jumps off and runs away."

"Yeah. Cats don't like to be picked up unless it's their idea," I explain.

"How was I supposed to know that?" Melissa asks, like it's my fault I didn't tell her before.

"Just pet your cat where she is. And stop petting her before she's tired of it," I tell her, hoping she really wants to help her cat.

"How am I supposed to know when she's tired of being petted?" Melissa whines.

"Watch her tail," I answer.

"For real?" Melissa asks, looking kind of interested now.

"If her tail is up," I explain, "your cat loves what you're doing. If her tail's down, not so much. If she arches her back or her fur stands up, back off fast."

"Cool. What are some other clues?" Alex asks.

Thank heaven for Alex. "Ears forward means your cat's on the offense. Ears back, defense. Whiskers forward might mean your cat's ready to attack. If she's aggravated at you, watch that tail move back and forth, faster and faster."

Alex asks me another question. Then Stephen asks one. Then Mikayla.

The clock gongs. I stop talking and listen. Eleven gongs. Hank has probably already told everybody that I'm not coming. He would have gotten to the courthouse early. He's early for everything. Hank can't stand to be late. I feel like a coward for not explaining things to Mom and Dad myself. But Hank will explain it better than I could anyway.

"Look at Berta," Stephen says.

I'm glad to get my mind out of the courtroom. "What's she doing?" I ask.

Some of the kids move so they can see Stephen's cat. Berta is lying on her back, legs in the air.

"She really trusts you, Stephen," I begin. "When a cat rolls over on her back like that, she's letting herself be vulnerable to you."

"Don't go there, Berta!" Cassie yells. "Been there, done that."

Everybody laughs. I'm probably the only one who didn't know Stephen and Cassie have history.

Stephen reaches for his cat's belly.

"Don't try to rub her belly or scratch her when she's like that," I warn. "She'll remember she's vulnerable, and she might scratch *you*."

"Exactly," Cassie says.

The room cracks up.

"Okay, okay," Fiona shouts. "That's enough."

"Don't we get to tell how our cats got better after we talked to Kat?" Mikayla asks. "Mine did."

"Mine too," Alex agrees.

Fiona ignores them. "Everybody just make

sure you've turned in your evaluations. Kat, cut to the chase."

I force myself to check the time. It's 11:15. I try not to think about the courtroom and what Hank's telling everybody. Maybe without me there, they can all be honest with the judge . . . and with themselves.

"So, what about my stupid cat?" Fiona demands. "Did you teach her anything?"

"Princess is *my* stupid cat," Arianna says. "Not yours. And who are you kidding? Nobody can teach that cat anything."

I've held on to Princess the whole time, partly because I thought it would be scary for her to maneuver around so many people and partly because holding her helped keep me together. "This week I discovered a lot about Princess," I begin.

Fiona sighs.

"I suspected something was wrong with her when she didn't meow. Then I noticed she didn't care about dogs barking or birds chirping."

"I know all that already," Fiona says.

Then I blurt it out. "Princess is blind. And deaf."

Somebody says, "You're kidding!"

Someone gasps.

Somebody else says, "That's so sad."

"Well, that's just great," Fiona says. "That pet store sold us a blind and deaf cat? They're going to hear from us, believe me."

"Now they *have* to take the cat back, right?" Arianna adds. "That's, like, false advertising or something."

"You can't take her back," I object.

"Just watch me," Fiona vows.

"But there's more, Fiona," I begin.

"What's left? The cat can't see, hear, or speak," Fiona complains. "She's going back to the pet store, and you can't change our minds."

"But she's a sweet cat. She'll love your family, and she'll let *you* love *her*."

"But we won't," Fiona says.

"No kidding," Arianna agrees. "Who wants a deaf, dumb, blind, and whatever cat?"

I don't understand how they can feel that way. I stroke Princess's head. Once I tell Fiona and Arianna that Princess is probably the only cat in Illinois who can use the john, it's got to change the way they feel about her. "Your cat is so smart, you guys. Wait till you hear what she can do."

Fiona rolls her eyes. "I'm waiting. And this better be good."

"Princess learned–" I stop. *This better be good?* "Wait. Why had this better be good?"

"Because the cat's going back to the pet store–or to the pound–if it's not. That's why," Fiona says.

And what if I tell them about their toilet-trained cat? What then? Why should that earn Princess a spot in this house? "Fiona, can't you love Princess as she is, for *who* she is?"

"I knew it," Fiona says. "You couldn't teach that cat to do anything, could you?"

"That's not what I'm saying," I answer. "I'm asking you why she *has* to do anything."

Fiona glares at me. "You know, I'm still not hearing any reason to keep that cat."

I look down at Princess lying in my arms. "Just because," I whisper, more to myself than to Fiona.

"What?" Fiona demands.

"Because," I repeat. And it feels like a revelation.

"Because? That's it? That's all?" Fiona laughs.

"Yep," I tell her, getting it myself at last. "That's all. Just because. Princess should have a home because she's Princess. That's all. She doesn't have to *do* anything. And guess what. Neither do I!"

"Fine," Fiona says. "I think we're done here."

For once, Fiona and I agree. We're done. "What time is it?" I ask.

Alex answers, "Um . . . 11:30." He walks up to me. "What are you going to do with Princess?"

I look at the cat, still asleep in my arms. "She's coming with me."

"Yes!" Alex whispers.

"Don't even think about bringing that cat back here," Fiona calls after me.

I dash out of the house, prepared to run to the courthouse with Princess in my arms.

A horn honks, and Hank opens the truck door. "About time," he calls.

"You waited?" I can't believe it. It must have killed Hank to sit out here, getting later and later. I hop in. "Thanks, Hank."

Hank takes back streets to the courthouse. The lot is almost empty. The courthouse is closed on Saturdays except for when they do adoptions. We park and run inside. Security at Nice Courthouse is a chubby security guard who goes to our church. He lets us in–with Princess–without any problem. But the girl at the front desk stops us cold.

"We're looking for the adoption judge, Judge Carroll," Hank tells her.

"First door on your right," she answers. "But you can't go in there with a cat."

I stick Princess inside my jacket and head back anyway while Hank works his magic on the girl. He catches up with me at the court-room door.

I stand on tiptoes and peek in. It's not the way I pictured a courtroom, more like a big office. On one side of the desk sits a thin man in a navy suit. On the other side, their backs to us, sit Mom, Dad, Dakota, and Wes. I reach for the doorknob, but Hank stops me.

"I know Judge Carroll," Hank says. "I called him when I knew we were going to be late. I told him what you told me, Kat."

"You promised, Hank."

"I promised I wouldn't tell Mom and Dad." He cracks the door and holds his finger over his lips. The judge looks up and nods at Hank. The others still have their backs to us.

". . . such a blessing to our family," Mom is saying. "I loved that girl from the first minute I saw her in the hospital. I thought the day we brought her to the farm was the happiest day of my life. But maybe this is. I just wish she were here with us."

"Mr. Coolidge?" the judge says.

"I second everything my Annie said," Dad answers. "I don't think I could go a day without seeing that angelic face, those eyes of hers. Sometimes I think Kat never let go of God's hand when she came down here. There's something so special about her."

I can't believe he said that, about God's hand.

The judge turns to Dakota.

"I'm not a Coolidge," she says, "so I don't get to vote or whatever you do here. But if I did, it would be a big thumbs-up for Kat. She taught me about family. And God. Kat's the reason I didn't run away from here. That kid deserves the best. And these guys are."

"What about me?" Wes snaps. "I've known Kat longer than Dakota."

"I'd love to hear from you, young man," the judge says.

"Okay. When I came to the Rescue, I was mad at everybody. Everything made me angry. Except Kat. I don't even know why. But it says something about her."

"Thank you for being so forthright, everyone. This isn't an official vote, of course. But I would like to ask you once more if you're sure you want to accept Katharine into your family, to give her the Coolidge name?"

"Yes!" They all shout it at the same time.

I can't take it any longer. I push through the door and into the arms of my family. "Me too!" I cry.

Hank joins the group hug. I think we're all crying. I look around at these people—my family. We're all holding hands: Mom, Dad, sisters, brothers . . . and God.

"Meow!"

I'd forgotten all about Princess, still stuffed inside my jacket.

"Is there a cat in my courtroom?" The judge stands up from his desk.

Princess meows again.

"Princess, you meowed!" I cry. I can hardly believe it. "You spoke!"

"It spoke?" the judge asks. "Now that's a first. And in *my* courtroom. I guess you better tell me what it said."

They're all staring at me, waiting for an answer. Then I get one. "I couldn't make out all of it, but it was something about *claw* and order."

Dad explodes in a bellow of a laugh that shakes the room. When he can speak, he beams at me. "Spoken like a true Coolidge."

Tips on Finding the Perfect Pet

- Talk with your whole family about owning a pet. Pets require a commitment from every member of the family. Your pet should be around for years—ten, fifteen, twenty, twenty-five, or thirty years, depending on the type of pet. Pets can be expensive, especially if they get sick or need medical care of any kind. Make sure you can afford to give your pet a good life for a long time.

- Think like your future pet. Would you be happy with the lifestyle in your house? Would you spend most of your time alone? Is there room for you in the house? If you're considering buying a horse, what kind of life will the horse have? Will someone be able to spend enough time caring for it?

- Study breeds and characteristics of the animal you're considering. Be prepared to spend time with your pet, bonding and training, caring and loving.

- Remember that there is no such thing as a perfect pet, just as there's no such thing as a perfect owner. Both you and your pet will need to work to develop the best possible relationship you can have and to become lifelong best friends.

Consider Pet Adoption

- Check out animal rescue organizations, such as the humane society (www.hsus.org), local shelters, SPCA (www.spca.com), 1-800-Save-A-Pet.com (PO Box 7, Redondo Beach, CA 90277), Pets911.com (great horse adoption tips), and Petfinder.com. Adopting a pet from a shelter will save that pet's life and make room for another animal, who might also find a good home.

- Take your time. Visit the shelters and talk with the animal care handlers. Legitimate shelters will be able to provide you with documentation on the animal's health and medical records. Find out all you can. Ask questions. Who owned the pet before? How many owners were there? Why was the pet given away? Is the pet housebroken? Does it like children?

- Consider adopting an adult pet. People tend to favor "babies," but adopting a fully grown animal may be less risky. What you see is what you get. The personality, size, and manners are there for you to consider.

Rescuing Animals

- It's great that you want to help every animal you meet. I wish everyone felt the same. But remember that safety has to come first. A frightened, abused animal can strike out at any time. If you find an animal that's in trouble, call your local animal shelter. Then try to find the owner.

- The best way to help a lost pet find its home again is to ask around. You might put a "Found Pet" ad in the paper or make flyers with the animal's picture on it. But be sure to report the find to your local shelter because that's where most owners will go for help in finding a lost pet.

- Report animal cruelty to your local animal shelter or to the humane society.

AUTHOR TALK

DANDI DALEY MACKALL grew up riding horses, taking her first solo bareback ride when she was three. Her best friends were Sugar, a Pinto; Misty, probably a Morgan; and Towaco, an Appaloosa. Dandi and her husband, Joe; daughters, Jen and Katy; and son, Dan, (when forced) enjoy riding Cheyenne, their Paint. Dandi has written books for all ages, including Little Blessings books, *Degrees of Guilt: Kyra's Story*, *Degrees of Betrayal: Sierra's Story*, *Love Rules*, *Maggie's Story*, and the best-selling series Winnie the Horse Gentler. Her books (about 450 titles) have sold more than 4 million copies. She writes and rides from rural Ohio.

Visit Dandi's Web site at
www.dandibooks.com

Can't get enough of Winnie? Visit her Web site to read more about Winnie and her friends plus all about their horses.

IT'S ALL ON WINNIETHEHORSEGENTLER.COM
There are so many fun and cool things to do on Winnie's Web site; here are just a few:

★ PAT'S PETS
Post your favorite photo of your pet and tell us a fun story about them

★ ASK WINNIE
Here's your chance to ask Winnie questions about your horse

★ MANE ATTRACTION
Meet Dandi and her horse, Cheyenne!

★ THE BARNYARD
Here's your chance to share your thoughts with others

★ AND MUCH MORE!